PUPPY PATROL

TEACHER'S PET

PUPPY PATROL
TEACHER'S PET

JENNY DALE

Illustrations by Mick Reid
Cover illustration by Michael Rowe

AN
APPLE
PAPERBACK

SCHOLASTIC INC.
New York Toronto London Auckland Sydney
Mexico City New Delhi Hong Kong

ISBN 0-439-11323-7

12 11 10   2 3 4/0

Printed in the U.S.A.   40
First Scholastic printing, October 1999

SPECIAL THANKS TO KAREN KING

PUPPY PATROL

TEACHER'S PET

CHAPTER ONE

The black-and-white Border collie stood very still, his ears pricked and his expression alert as he gazed down the track.

"What is it, Sam?" asked Neil Parker excitedly. He crouched down and put his head close to Sam's, straining into the sun to see exactly what it was that had caught his dog's attention. As far as he could make out, the wide trail ahead was empty. It was a popular route for people walking their dogs on weekends, but today Neil had thought they had it to themselves.

"I can't see anything, either," said his younger sister Emily, standing behind them both. She held a hand up to her face and squinted into the bright light. "Perhaps he's imagining things, or . . ."

"Wait! There. Look!" Neil pointed down the long

1

trail. A woman on a bicycle had just come into view, riding toward them. Then, from far off, they heard the sound of a dog barking. A large and energetic Dalmatian suddenly appeared, obviously chasing the bicycle.

"Sam's great, aren't you, Sam?" said Emily, ruffling the sleek coat behind his head. "I bet he could teach a few of the dogs in Dad's obedience classes a thing or two."

"You bet," agreed Neil proudly. "And some of the ones we have boarding!"

Bob and Carole Parker, Neil and Emily's parents, ran King Street Kennels — a boarding kennels and rescue center on the grounds of their house a couple of miles outside the nearby town of Compton. Dogs had been part of their family life for as long as Neil could remember — and he was crazy about them. It was his dream to work full-time with dogs himself when he was old enough.

The spotted Dalmatian was barking loudly as it bounded along the road toward them. The woman looked nervously over her shoulder, and her bicycle wobbled dangerously as the gap between her and the dog narrowed. Behind them, a man was running after them both, shouting desperately, "Dotty! Come here, girl!"

The Dalmatian completely ignored him. She caught up with the woman, leaping around alongside her, looking very pleased with herself.

Sam fidgeted with excitement and looked eager to join in the fun.

"No, Sam!" said Neil, firmly. "Stay!"

Sam immediately obeyed, sitting quietly, close to Neil's left leg.

"Dotty! Stop! Will you come here!" the man shouted over and over again. But Dotty continued to gallop alongside the woman on the bicycle, barking excitedly and snapping at the wheels.

Neil could see that the woman was extremely nervous. He recognized her now as Mrs. Smedley from the magazine store in Compton.

"It's OK, Mrs. Smedley!" he called to her. "Dalma-

tians are really friendly and playful! If you stop, she'll probably stop as well."

"I hope you're right," called Mrs. Smedley. She came to a halt beside Neil, looking anxiously down at the dog. The Dalmatian stopped, too, her big pink tongue hanging out, tail wagging, and a look of anticipation on her face.

"Dotty! Come here!" The man had reached them at last. Looking quite red in the face, and panting, he grabbed the leash hanging from his dog's collar. The Dalmatian immediately jumped up on him, covering his jacket with dirty pawprints. Staggering, the man lost his balance and fell backward into a muddy puddle, his legs spread-eagled in front of him.

"Oh, no!" they all cried. But dismay turned to smothered laughter as the silly Dalmatian began to lick the man's face enthusiastically. Even Mrs. Smedley smiled as the man squirmed in the mud, trying to fend off the dog's sloppy kisses.

"No, Dotty! Dotty, down!" he spluttered. At last he managed to push the dog away and get to his feet. Dotty promptly shook herself, sending specks of mud flying all over her owner's face and clothes.

It was the last straw. Brushing himself down as best he could, the man glared furiously at Neil and Emily, who were still grinning. Then he finally managed to attach the leash to the dog's collar and pulled her sharply toward him.

"I'm sorry if she frightened you," he said to Mrs.

Smedley. "I'm afraid Dotty can be rather playful. But she really wouldn't hurt anyone."

"I can see that." Mrs. Smedley smiled. "I hope you're all right, though."

"Yes, thank you," he replied stiffly. He turned to go and jerked at the leash again. "Come on, trouble!"

"What a fantastic dog!" Emily remarked as the man marched off with the Dalmatian.

"Yeah. Shame it's so out of hand, though," Neil replied. "Some people just have no idea how to train dogs."

Neil must have said it louder than he realized because the man turned around and glared at him again. He opened his mouth as if to say something, but before he could get a word out Dotty had raced off again, dragging her exhausted owner with her.

"Oh dear, the poor man!" chuckled Mrs. Smedley. "I'm afraid that dog is a bit too much to handle."

"Yeah, it certainly looks like it," Neil agreed. "Although my dad always says there's no such thing as a problem dog, Mrs. Smedley, only a problem owner!"

"I bet he feels awful, really," said Emily, always sympathetic toward people.

They all stood and watched until Dotty and her owner disappeared from view. Mrs. Smedley put her feet on the pedals of her bicycle and pushed off.

"Well, I'd better be on my way. See you both soon," she called over her shoulder.

Sam barked at Neil. He was eager to continue their morning walk after all the excitement.

"C'mon, Sam. Another ten minutes, then we'll turn back."

Sam sped away, eagerly darting around and sniffing at every familiar tree and bush, but always alert for commands from Neil.

As they approached the rear of the kennels, the sound of dogs barking reached them clearly. They had to leave the trail and cross a large, grassy meadow before jumping over the fence at the back of the kennels.

"What a racket!" said Emily. Luckily, the Parkers' house and kennels were set well away from the main road, where their nearest neighbors lived. King Street Kennels was always noisy, though: it showed just how popular they were. Some boarders came from up to twenty miles away.

Neil glanced at his watch. It was nine o'clock. "Feeding time!" he said, breaking into a run. "We can help out if we're quick. C'mon!"

Neil gave Sam a quick rubdown with a thick towel kept outside the back door and filled his drinking bowl with fresh water. As Sam retired to his favorite spot in the backyard underneath a leafy privet hedge, Neil and Emily headed across the courtyard and toward the first kennel block, where Carole Parker was busy preparing food for the boarding dogs.

"Where's Dad and Squirt?" asked Neil, using his favorite nickname for his five-year-old sister.

"Your father and *Sarah*," his mother replied, arching an eyebrow at him, "have gone into Compton to see Uncle Jack." She looked up from the clipboard on the feeding table where she was measuring some dry food into a dog bowl, ready to mix with water. "I think he said he was going to get that video from Steve, too. He knew you wanted it." She pushed a stray lock of her short black hair out of her eyes and took a can from the shelf above the table. She was a strikingly tall woman, dressed in brown cords and a loose sweatshirt.

"Great." Neil was always borrowing things from his cousin, Steve Tansley. He usually spent all of his own pocket money on books and magazines about dogs. "Can we help?"

"Yes, indeed. Why don't you go and join Kate in Block Two? Thanks, Neil," said his mother, placing another dog bowl on the table and checking her clipboard again. She emptied the can of dog food into it and mixed it with some dry dog food. The dogs were all kept to the diet they were fed at home, which often meant mixing lots of different meals. "Emily, you and I can finish here."

Neil crossed the courtyard to Kennel Block Two. The door was open, so he walked in and looked around for Kate McGuire, their kennel assistant. Both kennel blocks consisted of two rows of ten pens on either side, with individual sleeping quarters in each, and a central aisle.

The large inside pens were light and airy, and heating pipes set in tunnels in the concrete floor kept the kennels cozy in the winter. A lever on the outside of the pen controlled the door that gave the dogs access to the large wire mesh runs outside. Each pen generally had a personal touch, as owners insisted on bringing their pet's own basket or blanket from home and some favorite toys.

Neil soon found Kate with Buttons, an adorable little black-and-white, rough-coated mongrel. Buttons had two comical black ears perched on top of her head, and bright, friendly eyes. Her owners, Mr. and Mrs. Timms, lived just outside Compton. They had brought her to the kennels the day before and were now on their way to America for a three-week vacation.

Kate's long blonde hair was up in a ponytail, and she wore her usual baggy sweatshirt and leggings. "Poor Buttons. She's really sad," she told Neil. "Won't touch her food at all."

Buttons was lying listlessly with her head on her paws. Sad eyes gazed down at the ground.

"She's lost her sparkle since yesterday, hasn't she?" Neil said thoughtfully. "Come on, girl, cheer up!" He went over and stroked her gently. "You'll be fine here."

Buttons closed her eyes and sighed deeply.

"I'll leave the food down for a while. She'll probably eat it later," Kate decided.

Neil closed the pen behind them, gazing anxiously
at the sad little dog. Sometimes dogs did miss their
owners at first, but they usually settled down once
they got used to the routine of the kennels and to the
love and attention that the Parkers and Kate gave
them.

In the pen next to Buttons was Jed, a huge fawn-
colored Great Dane with a gentle nature and an
enormous appetite. The large bowl of food Kate put
down for him disappeared in seconds.

Then came Sally, a tricolored basset hound who
was very much at home at King Street Kennels.
She'd visited plenty of times, as her owners often
had to go abroad. As soon as Neil opened her pen,
Sally rolled over on to her back with her legs in the
air, eager to have her tummy tickled. Neil remembered how sad Sally had been when she first came to
the kennels a few years ago. He felt sure Buttons
would soon feel just as much at home.

Kate fed the last of the dogs. Ruff was a golden retriever who was due to go home the following day.
He'd attached himself to Kate right away and sulked
if anyone else fed him.

"Well, I'm done until Monday," she said, closing the
pen door. "You're back in school then, aren't you,
Neil?"

"Yeah, lucky me!" Neil grimaced. He'd really enjoyed spending so much time at the kennels during the long summer vacation. "We've got a new teacher and I'm dreading it!"

"Oh, it's always like that to start with," said Kate, sympathetically. "Don't worry, I'm sure you'll be fine."

Neil hoped so. Mrs. Oakham, who had been his teacher until she left last term, had always encouraged his interest in dogs. It was probably too much to hope that her replacement would be as understanding.

CHAPTER TWO

"**C**ome on, Neil. We'll be late!" Emily shouted toward the kennels from the back door of the house. She always liked to get to school in time to chat with her friends before going in to class. The first day of school was especially important.

"OK, I'm coming!"

Neil was crouching beside Buttons, stroking her head. She had been sad for the rest of the weekend, refusing most of her food and moping in her basket. She hadn't even ventured into her outside run.

"I'll be back soon," he whispered as he stood up. With one last glance at the sad little dog he firmly closed the pen door after him and ran across the courtyard to the house.

"Hurry up!" called their mother. She was waiting outside on the driveway in their green Range Rover. Neil could see Emily and Sarah already in the backseat.

Usually Neil would bike the couple of miles to school with Chris Wilson, his best friend, who lived a little farther along the main road. Although they were the same age and were both short, with dark brown spiky hair, they had some very different interests.

Today, however, Neil had wanted to spend time with Buttons — even if it meant arriving at school with his sisters.

*   *   *

"Well, I hope you all like your new classes," said Mrs. Parker as she pulled up alongside the entrance to Meadowbank School.

"I just hope my new teacher's as good as Mrs. Oakham," said Neil, opening the door and jumping out.

Mrs. Parker gave Sarah a quick kiss and waved to Neil and Emily. "Bye. I'll see you all later this afternoon."

"Hey! The Puppy Patrol's arrived!" quipped a familiar voice as they walked through the school gates.

Neil turned and smiled at Hasheem, the class joker. He was used to his friends and other people in the town referring to them as the "Puppy Patrol." The name had stuck because they were seen around Compton so often in their Range Rover with its King Street Kennels logo.

"Hi, Hasheem. What's new?" he asked.

"Nothing much. Except our new teacher is friendly, easygoing, and doesn't believe in homework . . ." Hasheem grinned.

"Really?" said Neil, falling for Hasheem's serious tone.

"In your dreams!" laughed Hasheem.

Neil punched his arm playfully.

When they walked into the classroom, their new teacher was already there, writing on the board. He had his back to the class but something about him struck Neil as familiar. When the teacher turned around, Neil gasped in dismay. It was the owner of the Dalmatian they had met on Saturday!

The teacher's gaze fell on Neil and his face reddened slightly. Obviously, he remembered Neil, too.

"Be seated, please," the teacher commanded briskly. "And no talking!"

He looked at Neil coldly, as if his remarks were solely for Neil's benefit.

Just my luck! Neil thought bitterly as he walked to his desk. *Of all the people in the world, our new teacher has to be him!*

Once they had all taken their seats, they could see the words MR. HAMLEY written in block capitals on the blackboard.

"Good morning, everyone. As you can see, my name is Mr. Hamley," he said. "In a minute I'll ask you all to introduce yourselves. But first I want to make one thing crystal clear: You are here to learn, and I am here to teach you. I will not tolerate any time-wasting or bad behavior in my class."

His steely gaze swept over the sea of faces in front of him, then rested on Neil, his eyes narrowing. "Is that understood?"

Something tells me I'm a marked man, Neil thought uncomfortably.

When it was Neil's turn to stand up and introduce

himself, Mr. Hamley repeated his name as if committing it to memory.

This was just the start to a new term Neil *didn't* need.

Neil felt jittery all morning and was relieved when it was time for recess. He couldn't wait to see Chris and give him the news!

Chris ran his fingers through his thick hair and whistled. "Wow, that's really tough luck. But maybe he'll loosen up after a couple of days."

"I hope so," sighed Neil. "But I'm not going to hold my breath. You should have seen him looking at me. I'm definitely not his favorite pupil right now!"

The rest of the class weren't too impressed either.

"Man, it's just our luck to get landed with a monster without a sense of humor," said Hasheem. "I thought I was finished!"

Mr. Hamley had asked if anyone knew where the United Nations sat and Hasheem's reply "On chairs, sir!" had resulted in a withering look and a threat of extra homework.

"If he smiled he'd crack his face!" said one of the others.

"And he's really got it in for you, hasn't he?" Hasheem asked, turning to Neil. "What have you done to rattle his cage?"

So the other kids *had* noticed. Neil shrugged his

shoulders. He thought it best not to mention the episode with the Dalmatian. "Maybe he just doesn't like my face!" he replied, trying to laugh. If Mr. Hamley knew Neil had told the rest of the class about Saturday, he'd be even more annoyed. Neil just hoped his new teacher would forget all about it sooner rather than later.

But Mr. Hamley's mood didn't improve. He frowned all day and his manner was very abrupt. Especially with Neil. Neil breathed a sigh of relief when the bell rang for the end of school.

Thankfully, Neil shrugged on his jacket and walked out of the school building. He could see the Range Rover parked across the street, and hurried over.

His father was in the driver's seat this time. Bob Parker was a very large man and had short brown hair not unlike Neil's. He was wearing one of his green sweatshirts that had the King Street Kennels logo across the chest. Sarah and Emily were already sitting in the back, grumbling at Sam who was climbing all over them, trying to reach Neil.

Neil made a huge fuss over the collie.

"Hi! How's Buttons, Dad?" Neil asked as he fastened his seat belt. "Is she any better?"

"No, she's not much happier," replied his father, slipping the car into gear. "But it's still early. It's the first time she's been away from home, so she's bound to feel nervous. I'm sure she'll perk up in a day or two."

"And guess what, Neil," Emily said. "There's a new dog at the rescue center!"

"Is there, Dad? What breed is it? Where did you find it?"

"Hang on, one question at a time," Bob Parker smiled. "Yes, we have got another dog. Someone found him wandering around in the woods. No collar, a bit skinny, obviously hungry, and very frightened."

"Just like Sam," said Emily. "Remember?"

Neil had been seven when the poor, weak puppy was found abandoned and brought to the rescue center. It didn't take much to persuade his parents to break their own rule and to keep Sam as the family pet, either.

The rescue center had ten pens for strays but only two were occupied at the moment — by Diamond, a beautiful Afghan hound whose owners had gotten tired of grooming her, and Max, a black-and-tan mongrel who had almost certainly been dumped — perhaps when his owners went on vacation — without a collar to identify him.

"If people don't want their pets, why don't they find them another home instead of abandoning them?"

"It makes me angry, too, Neil," his father told him quietly. "But that's why your mom and I started the rescue center in the first place. It's good to be able to help these dogs and find them a new home if we can."

"Can we go and see the dog when we get back, Daddy?" Sarah piped up.

"Yes, but don't go in the pen, honey," Mr. Parker replied. "He's very nervous and jumpy. He needs some rest and quiet and time to settle down. OK?"

Mr. Parker turned the car into their gravel driveway and pulled up. The three children piled out and hurried over to the rescue center, a small block set aside from the main kennels.

Their mother was there, filling in a form with details about the new dog. It was important to note the stray's description and where and when he was found, in case the owner turned up to claim him.

"I suppose you've come to see the new arrival?" she asked, smiling at them.

"Can we?" Neil asked.

"Of course. But remember he's been living rough for a while so he doesn't look too good. And he's very nervous, so don't alarm him."

She led them to the last pen where a thin, sandy-colored mongrel was lying in the corner. It stood, hackles raised as they approached, and growled.

"Poor thing," said Emily softly. "He's all skin and bones!"

"Not for long," her mother reassured her. "He's so wary of us, though, I'd guess he's been treated badly at some time."

The dog looked neglected and frightened.

"It's all right, boy, we won't hurt you," said Neil gently, crouching down outside the pen, but the dog backed into the farthest corner of the enclosure and snarled at him.

The pens in the rescue center were pretty much the same as the ones in the boarding kennel blocks, but a bit smaller, and with basic plastic dog baskets for easy cleaning. Like the others, there was an outside run, too.

The center was mostly maintained with the help of money from the local county government and the occasional fund-raising event put on by friends.

The Parkers would nurse mistreated or sick dogs back to full health and then try to find them new, more responsible owners.

"What should we call him?" asked Sarah.

"How about Growler?" suggested Emily.

Neil shook his head. "He won't always be a growler, Em," he said. "Let's call him Sandy."

"Sandy it is, then," said their mother, writing the name down on her form. "Let him settle in, now. You three go and get changed. You'll find some snacks in the kitchen."

"Well, how was your first day back at school?" Carole Parker asked as they all sat around the large wooden kitchen table waiting for Bob to serve the dinner. It was his turn to cook the meal tonight.

"Great!" said Emily. "Mrs. Rowntree made me Rabbit Monitor."

"Rabbit Monitor?" asked her dad. "Does that mean you have to keep counting them?"

There was laughter around the table.

"No, silly! I have to look after them with Angie Smith. You know, feed them and stuff."

"And I suppose it means you have to bring them home on vacations?" said her mother with a wry look at her husband.

"Well, I don't know. We haven't got any yet."

More laughter, even louder. Emily flushed, but had to grin as well.

"There's no need to laugh. Mrs. Rowntree says we can get a couple later in the semester, when we start learning about them."

"I got two stars for my picture!" said Sarah, then beamed with pleasure at everyone's congratulations. She loved drawing and painting.

"How about you, Neil?" his father asked, placing a bowl of hot spaghetti on the table in front of him.

Neil's smile faded. "Don't ask," he said. "Our new teacher, Mr. Hamley, is really strict. He's got no sense of humor, and he's *already* got it in for me."

His parents exchanged worried glances.

"Why? What happened?" asked his mother with concern.

Neil described the incident with Mr. Hamley and Dotty the Dalmatian on Saturday. "I didn't mean for him to hear what I said about people who don't know how to train their dogs," he explained. "But he did hear it and I suppose it upset him."

Bob Parker looked thoughtful. "The poor man's probably feeling very embarrassed. And worried, maybe, that you won't respect him or that he'll be laughed at if you tell the rest of the class about him. Not the best way for a new teacher to start off, is it?"

Neil nodded. Dad could always make him see things from another person's point of view and that wasn't always easy to accept.

"So what should I do now?" Neil asked. "How can I convince him I'm not out to cause trouble?"

"Work hard and try to forget what happened last Saturday," advised Carole Parker. "This will soon blow over. When he's settled in a bit more and gotten to know you, I'm sure you'll both get along fine."

Neil hoped his parents were right.

CHAPTER THREE

The next morning Sarah came rushing downstairs looking excited.

"I've done it!" she announced triumphantly. "I've taught Fudge to sit."

Fudge was her pet hamster. Sarah knew he was the cleverest hamster in the world, and was always trying to train him to do tricks. Even the fact that hamsters like to sleep a lot during the day didn't deter her. As soon as Fudge poked his head out of his house for a quick drink or nibble at his food, Sarah seized him for another training session before he could go to sleep again.

"Get real, Sarah, you can't teach a hamster to do anything," Emily told her, rolling her eyes in mock exasperation.

"Yes, you can!" Sarah replied. "I told Fudge to sit and he did. So there!"

Neil looked up from his breakfast cereal and grinned at his sisters. It was no use telling Sarah that Fudge only sat because he wanted to. She'd never believe it.

"That's very good, Sarah," smiled Bob Parker. "Keep at it and you'll soon be able to take Fudge out without a leash!"

"Oh, but . . ." Sarah suddenly frowned as she realized her dad was teasing her. The others laughed loudly.

"Oh, you!" she said and stomped out again.

The doorbell rang.

"That'll be Chris," said Neil.

He grabbed a piece of toast off the table and picked up his schoolbag on the way out. "See y'later."

"Neil! Your hair!" his mother called after him.

Neil grunted and smoothed his hand over his spiky hair, which always seemed to be a mess. He gave a quick good-bye pat to Sam and grabbed his bike.

Chris was waiting in the driveway for him. "What kept you?" he asked. "I thought you weren't coming for a minute!"

"I wish I wasn't," Neil told him. "I'm not looking forward to another day with Hamley. I wish I was in your class."

"Maybe he'll be in a better mood today," Chris said as they set off.

Somehow Neil doubted that.

The two boys rode through the school gates and over to the bicycle sheds. They locked up their bikes and went over to join a group of friends before classes started.

"Hope you're ready for another fun-filled day with Smiler," Hasheem said to Neil.

Neil chuckled. "Just don't make any more wise-cracks," he warned him.

"Who? Me?" replied Hasheem with wide-eyed innocence. "Would I ever?"

To Neil's relief, their teacher seemed in a slightly better mood today.

"This morning I want you all to write about yourselves," Mr. Hamley told the class. "Tell me about your families, your hobbies, what you want to do when you leave school. Anything you like. That way I'll get to know you all better."

There was the usual clatter of desk lids, sighs, and rustling of notebooks, but eventually the room was silent apart from the occasional cough or sneeze and the creak of chair legs.

Neil set about describing King Street Kennels, and his experience with Sam and the other dogs. The words flowed. This was his passion, after all. He was always at his best when he was writing or talking about what he loved most. When the bell rang for recess, he looked up dazed. Where had the time gone? He felt quite pleased with his work and just hoped Mr. Hamley would like it, too!

That afternoon when Neil got home, he saw Emily playing their version of soccer with Sam in the courtyard behind the house. Immediately, Sam lost all interest in the game and ran over to greet Neil joyfully.

"Hello, Sam!" Neil bent down to pat the dog roughly and playfully. Sam almost seemed to laugh with pleasure. He pushed his head at Neil and pretended to chew the boy's hand.

"Want to play?" Emily asked.

"Sure," he nodded. "But Chris'll be here soon. Let's wait for him, then we can go over to the field."

Chris arrived a few minutes later and they set off with Sam, a well-chewed ball, and some sweatshirts for goalposts. Once in the field behind the kennels, they divided into two teams — Neil and Sam against Chris and Emily — and kicked off.

"The ball, Sam! Tackle the ball!" Neil shouted as the Border collie ran after Chris, who was dribbling the ball toward the goal. Sam caught up with Chris, pounced on the ball, and nosed it away toward Neil. Neil kicked it toward the goal but it just fell short.

"Goal, Sam!" Neil called as Emily raced over to defend. Sam cut in front of her and charged be-

tween the two sweatshirts, pushing the ball ahead of him.

"*Goal! Yeah!* Way to go, Sam!" yelled Neil, jumping up and punching the air in triumph.

Sam barked and ran around excitedly.

"We need a new rule," said Chris, gasping for breath. "No touching the ball with your nose allowed!"

"I don't think there's much that dog can't do!" laughed Mr. Parker, who had been watching them. He leaned his arms on the top rail of the fence.

Sam was now dancing around Neil, barking for the game to go on. Neil bent down to pat him, then turned to his father. "He's really great, isn't he?"

"Well, he should be — you've been training him since he was a puppy," Chris reminded him.

Bob Parker stroked his chin thoughtfully. "You know, I've heard they're going to include a special Agility event at the county show this year. It's at the end of this month. Why don't you enter Sam? It would be good experience for him — and you!"

"What's agility?" asked Emily.

"It's a kind of obstacle course that dogs have to run around against the clock," explained Bob.

"Wow! Sam would be great at that. Go for it!" said Chris.

Neil looked at them both, wondering, then down at Sam who was looking up at him, tongue lolling.

"How about that, Sam?" asked Neil, fondling Sam's ears. Sam barked with enthusiasm. He could tell by Neil's voice that something exciting was in the air. "You could probably do something like that with your eyes shut, couldn't you?" Sam's tail wagged furiously.

The county show was held on the fairgrounds near Compton every year. It was a huge event and attracted crowds of people.

"I'd bet on him, anyway," said Chris.

"Hey, that's an idea. Why don't we get people to sponsor him to complete the course?" suggested Neil. "We could raise some money for the rescue center."

"No, let's send the money to the SPCA for a change," suggested Emily. "They help all animals, all over the country." She was a member of several animal support societies and was always looking at ways to raise funds for them. "We could do that, couldn't we, Dad?" she asked.

"I don't see why not. We'd have to arrange it properly of course and get some official sponsor forms from the SPCA." He nodded approvingly. "But yes, I think it's a very good idea. I'll check out the details of the show. There are rules for these things, and you probably have to register early."

"And I'll be the first sponsor," offered Chris.

Back at the kennels, they found Kate just finishing in Block Two.

"How's Buttons, Kate?" asked Mr. Parker.

Kate looked a bit worried. "Still very low, Bob. And She's hardly touched her food again."

"We'll get Mike to look at her when he calls tomorrow, just to be on the safe side," said Mr. Parker. Mike Turner was their local vet from nearby Padsham. He came to check on the dogs twice a week, or when there was any emergency.

"How about Sandy?" asked Neil. "Is he any friendlier, Kate?"

"Not really. He still won't let me get near him," Kate replied.

"We'll go and take a look at him," said Bob. He turned to Neil and the others. "But remember, don't come in the pen unless I tell you to."

"OK. Are you coming, Em?"

"No way! That dog scares me," she confessed. "Anyway, I want to see Mom about sponsoring Sam for the show."

"I've got to go, too," said Chris. "See you tomorrow, Neil. Bye, everyone."

Emily took Sam with her while Neil and his father headed over to the rescue center.

Sandy was lying in his basket. As soon as he saw them approaching, he jumped out and crouched in a corner, growling softly and quivering.

Mr. Parker spoke gently to him as he opened the pen. He walked slowly over to the dog.

Sandy bared his teeth and snarled louder. He looked ready to attack. Neil watched anxiously outside the cage, keeping very still so as not to alarm the dog. He knew his father was very good with dogs, but this one looked really fierce and unapproachable. Almost like a wild animal.

Still talking, Bob Parker stood very still and slowly took a couple of small dogs treats out of his pocket. He placed them on the floor between him and Sandy.

"There now, good boy," he said quietly, and slowly backed out of the pen.

"I was a bit worried there for a moment," Neil admitted as his father shut the kennel door. "Do you think he would have gone for you?"

"If he felt threatened. That's why you mustn't go in the pen yet. This dog has been very badly treated by someone and it's going to take him a long time to trust anyone again."

Neil looked anxiously at Sandy.

Even Sam had never been this bad.

Chris called after dinner to say that his mom and dad had offered to sponsor Sam in the county show, too.

"That's great," said Emily when she heard.

Mrs. Parker had been delighted at the whole idea and had readily agreed to write to the SPCA for sponsor forms. "Why don't you ask Mrs. Smedley if you can leave a sponsor form in the magazine store?" she suggested over the top of her newspaper. "I'm sure a lot of people in the town would sign up, too."

"Hey, we could call him the Puppy Patrol dog," said Emily. "That'd be cool! Great publicity for the kennels, too."

"Sponsor the Puppy Patrol dog — yeah, I like it." Neil nodded.

"It's not fair. I want to enter Fudge in the show, too," Sarah pouted.

"There's a cleverest pet competition, Sarah," her father told her. "You can enter Fudge in that."

Sarah's face lit up. "Oh, good! In that case, I'll have to go and start on his training as soon as he wakes up!" she said seriously. "I should be able to get him to beg as well as sit, in time for the show."

There were snorts and chokes from the others as they tried to suppress their laughter, but Sarah ignored them and left the room.

"Poor Fudge — he won't get a minute's peace now!" laughed Carole Parker.

"Maybe I'd better start a training schedule for Sam, too," said Neil.

"I can help, if you want," offered Emily. "We want to make sure Sam does well against all the other dogs!"

"Well, there's one dog you won't have to worry

about," his mother told him. "And that's your teacher's Dalmatian. From what you say, he won't be entering her in any obedience competitions!"

"You're right," said Neil, suddenly chilled by the memory of that awful encounter. "That would take a real miracle!"

CHAPTER FOUR

Neil was so excited about the coming show that he found it difficult to concentrate on his schoolwork the next day. Reluctantly, he tore his thoughts away from his daydream of Sam being presented with the trophy for first prize and started doing the work his class had been assigned.

He had felt Mr. Hamley's eyes on him a few times that morning and it made him nervous. Was Smiler still angry with him?

Then, just as he was leaving the classroom for lunch, Mr. Hamley called out to him. "I'd like a word with you, please, Neil."

"Uh-oh. There may be trouble ahead!" sang Hasheem softly as Neil turned back.

Neil walked over to his teacher's desk, trying not to look nervous.

"Yes, sir?"

Neil could see Mr. Hamley was reading his essay about King Street Kennels. He bit his lip. Was it awful?

"I found your essay very interesting, Neil."

Relief flooded through Neil. He wasn't in trouble, after all. He relaxed slightly and discovered he'd been clutching the strap of his schoolbag in a death grip without realizing it.

"Especially this bit about your father's obedience classes," Mr. Hamley continued. He gave Neil an awkward smile. "As you know, I have a rather unruly Dalmatian. My wife and I have been trying to train Dotty for some time, but without much success. In fact, we've almost given up hope. So I wondered if your father would help us train Dotty."

Neil grinned hugely. He could hardly believe his ears.

"Of course he would, sir! Do you want me to ask him tonight?" he asked eagerly.

Mr. Hamley smiled. *He didn't look half so fierce when he relaxed a bit,* Neil thought. *His eyes sort of twinkled.*

"Thank you, but I think it would be better if I called your father myself," he replied. "Can you give me the number? I'll get in touch with him tonight."

Neil left the classroom walking on air. This was better than he dared hope. His dad would teach Dotty to be obedient in no time! Then perhaps Mr. Hamley would forget about their first encounter.

Chris was waiting for him outside school, looking worried.

"Hasheem said Mr. Hamley kept you behind," he said. "What's the problem?"

Neil shook his head and told Chris about his conversation with their teacher.

"Wow! Your dad's going to train that crazy dog?" Chris raised his eyebrows in surprise. "That'll be something!"

Neil found his father in the kennel office when he got home from school and told him to expect a call from Mr. Hamley.

"I'm looking forward to meeting this Dalmatian," said Mr. Parker. "She sounds like quite a challenge."

"She is! Mr. Hamley said he's been trying to train her for a long time."

He bent down to greet Sam, who had nudged open the office door to come and find him. "And I'd better start practicing with you, shouldn't I, Sam? The county show's only a few weeks away."

Sam wagged his tail eagerly. If Neil was excited, then Sam was, too!

"I've been reading about Agility courses in my dog books," said Neil to his father. "Can we use some things from the storeroom to make an obstacle course in the field?"

"Help yourself. But make sure there's nothing Sam can hurt himself on. That reminds me — I haven't found those application forms yet. We must get you both registered."

"OK. Come on, Sam." Neil ran across to the storeroom between the two kennel blocks with Sam bounding beside him.

"Hey, Em!" he shouted, seeing his sister in the garden. "D'you want to help me make an Agility course for Sam?"

"Sure." Emily ran over to join him. "Loads of people were interested in it at school today. He's sure to get plenty of sponsors. He'll raise stacks of money for the SPCA if he completes the course."

"You'll do better than that, won't you, boy?"

Sam wagged his tail and barked.

"See!" laughed Neil. "He agrees!"

Inside the storeroom they found some small steps, a few planks of wood, an empty food barrel with top and bottom lids removed, and an old tire.

Armed with these and some bricks to help build the jumps, they soon made a makeshift course in the nearby field. Then Neil took Sam through his paces.

Sam looked a bit puzzled at first, but Neil ran around the course with him as he would on the big day itself, showing him what to do, and the dog made a fantastic effort to obey. Crawling through the bar-

rel caused some hilarious moments, but to Sam it was all a wonderful game.

"Well done, Sam." Emily clapped as the Border collie ran along the simple seesaw they had made with a plank and two bricks. This was probably the most difficult item on the course, since Sam had to make it tilt once he got to the center and not jump off too soon.

Neil rewarded him with a favorite treat, and Sam looked ready to do it all over again.

"No, Sam. That'll do for today," Neil said. His dad had always told him to finish a training session when a dog had been successful at something, so you could praise him. That way he'd be happy to work with you again.

Neil glanced at his watch. It was five-thirty. Mr. Hamley had probably called by now. He and Emily hurried over to the office to find out.

Mr. Parker was talking on the telephone.

"We'll see you at seven-thirty then," he was saying.

Neil sat in his mother's swivel chair at her desk, while his dad finished the conversation. He couldn't resist spinning around just once.

"Was that Mr. Hamley?" asked Neil eagerly, as soon as his father had replaced the receiver. "Is he bringing Dotty tonight?"

"Yes, and I think it's going to be an interesting challenge," Mr. Parker said. "Apparently, Mrs. Hamley is expecting a baby so they've been trying to get their Dalmatian trained before the baby arrives. Dotty is very high-spirited and they've already had to take her away from three schools in disgrace."

"From what I saw of her on Saturday I'm not surprised," said Neil. "But *you* can straighten her out, can't you, Dad? You can work miracles with any dog!"

His father laughed at Neil's faith in him. "Thanks for the vote of confidence, but training is just as much for the owner, you know. It's important that the dog knows who's boss. Dogs are pack animals, Neil. They have to look at their owners as pack leaders, or they won't obey them."

Well, Dotty certainly didn't look at Mr. Hamley as her boss, Neil thought. *Still, Dad would soon straighten that out.*

Suddenly an awful thought struck him. What if Dotty never improved? Would he and Mr. Hamley be back at square one?

"Can I stay and watch the obedience class tonight?" he asked eagerly.

"I've got a better idea," his father said. "I'd be glad if you'd help me out. There are two long-haired dachshunds coming tonight — Candy and Honey — and I could do with an extra handler for one of them. But if that Dalmatian acts up, don't laugh, OK? You don't want to upset Mr. Hamley again, do you?"

"I won't," Neil promised. He was delighted his dad had asked him to help. "Can I go and see Buttons and Sandy now?"

"Dinner first. Then you can do the rounds with me before the lesson starts."

After dinner, Neil and his father went to check on the dogs. It was a warm night, still light, and the dogs were all out in their runs. All except Buttons. She was still lying in her basket.

"Well, at least she's drunk the glucose water the vet gave her this morning," Bob said. "He gave her a vitamin shot, too. That should perk her up a bit."

Over in the rescue center, Sandy growled at their approach and once again backed into the far corner, watching them warily.

"He's still scared," said Neil.

"Yes. And it will probably take him a while to realize he's safe here." Mr. Parker turned to Neil. "So promise me — no going in the pen for now, OK?"

"I promise, Dad. But can I give him something?" Neil always kept a couple of doggy treats in his pocket for Sam. "I'll put it through the wire."

Mr. Parker nodded. "Go on, then."

Neil pushed the food through the wire mesh. It landed on the floor just in front of the ragged animal.

"Here you are, Sandy." Neil spoke very gently to him. "Come on, boy. Don't be scared."

Sandy growled softly, his eyes fixed on the treat in front of him.

"Let's move back," suggested Mr. Parker. "Then he might take it."

Sandy eyed them warily as they backed away, then trotted over and, still watching them, snapped up the biscuit.

"Good boy!" Neil encouraged him warmly, but Sandy had already scuttled back into the corner.

"Let's leave him now," said Mr. Parker. "I'll look in on him again later."

"Hey, it's nearly time for the obedience class to start," said Neil, checking his watch.

"I know. Everything's just about ready." Mr. Parker usually held his classes in a large converted barn on one side of their property.

As they walked back they heard the office bell ring. Mr. Parker opened the gate at the side of the house. It was Mr. Hamley, holding his Dalmatian on a leash.

"Hello, sir!" Neil smiled, reaching down to stroke the dog. "Hello, Dotty!"

Up close, she really was a beautiful animal and in the peak of health. Neil guessed that she was probably about eighteen months old. Her gleaming white coat was peppered with black spots. Black, silky ears framed her elegant face.

"Dotty looks beautiful," said Mr. Parker. "You obviously care for her very well indeed." He squatted down and Dotty received his gentle stroking with interest and a wagging tail.

"Thank you. She has her moments though. I just hope she doesn't misbehave tonight." Mr. Hamley still looked tense.

"If she does, she won't be on her own," said Mr. Parker. "My nephew, Steve, is bringing his Labrador, Ricky, and we can always rely on him to disobey orders!"

Mr. Hamley's face relaxed a little. "Sounds like they'll be a good pair, then."

They were interrupted by loud barking as the other dogs began to arrive and greet one another enthusiastically.

At the front of the group was Ricky, who had cast an eager eye at Dotty and decided he liked what he saw. He was barking and pulling at his leash, trying to drag Neil's thirteen-year-old cousin, Steve, over to his new friend.

"No, Ricky! Heel!" Steve was shouting, to no effect. The golden Labrador was a short but solid, powerful dog. Slightly built Steve was no match for him.

"Ricky! Sit!" Mr. Parker commanded, loudly and firmly. The golden Labrador immediately sat down and looked at him, ears raised, listening for the next command.

"I don't know how you do it, Uncle Bob," said Steve, shaking his head and out of breath. "Ricky never does that for me."

"Well, I hope you have the same success with Dotty," remarked Mr. Hamley, greatly impressed by the simple demonstration.

"Let's go and find out," said Mr. Parker.

CHAPTER FIVE

Seven boisterous young dogs and their owners packed into the barn. Ricky and Dotty both managed to tangle their leashes in their efforts to play and make friends.

Mr. Hamley looked embarrassed, but Steve was laughing. He was used to Ricky's antics. Catching Neil's eye, he raised his eyebrows in mock despair as he bent down to untangle the two dogs.

Neil grinned. He loved these sessions. Most of the dogs were fairly unruly at first but gradually, as the lessons progressed under his dad's expert coaching, they all became much better behaved. It was a bonus if his dad gave him a dog to handle as well.

"Hello, everyone. Thank you all for coming," Mr. Parker said in a loud, friendly voice. "I hope you enjoy the lesson. Training your dog should be fun as well as rewarding." He smiled as he looked around the barn at the assortment of dogs and their owners. "I believe that a well-trained dog is a happy dog, and a pleasure to its owner. If you follow instructions and practice the work we do here, there's no reason why your dog shouldn't be well behaved."

Ricky barked loudly and Mr. Parker grinned at him.

"Yes, even you, Ricky!"

There was a ripple of laughter as Ricky barked again, as if in agreement.

"Now, there's one thing I'm going to draw to your attention before we start." He held up a crumpled plastic bag. "The dog owner's most important equipment after the voice and the leash!"

Neil smiled — he'd heard this speech before — and noticed that some of the owners were looking baffled while others seemed to know what was coming.

"Never go out for a walk with your dog without one of these in your pocket to clean up after him! It's not only the law now, but it's also responsible consideration for the environment and other people — and for your dog, who can't clean up after himself even if he wanted to!"

More laughter. Point made.

"Let's start off by getting your dogs to walk to heel," continued Mr. Parker. He demonstrated how they should hold their leashes correctly. "I'd like you all to walk your dogs around the barn now, please. If you'd like to go first, Steve?" He nodded at his nephew.

Steve started walking with Ricky bounding along-side him. Behind them was Bella the Gordon setter, pulling ahead eagerly. Then Candy, one of the long-haired dachshunds, who was busily sniffing the ground and darting suddenly off the track in all directions.

Neil followed with Honey, her littermate. She was much quieter than Candy and trotted sweetly along-side Neil, gazing up at him with button-black eyes as if making sure she was doing everything properly. Behind them came Scamp, a bouncy Old English

sheepdog puppy with a nature true to his name, and finally Lady, a lovable little Yorkshire terrier, owned by Mrs. Swinton, a neighbor of Steve's.

But where was Dotty? Neil looked around, puzzled. Then he saw her, stretched out on the floor of the barn, refusing to budge. Mr. Hamley was pulling ineffectually on her leash and calling her quietly, trying to make her stand, but Dotty was completely ignoring him. Neil smothered a grin. Trust Dotty!

Mr. Parker strolled casually over to them.

"Dotty! Get up, girl!" Mr. Hamley whispered, his face red with embarrassment. "Come on, get up!"

"Having a bit of trouble, Paul?" asked Mr. Parker.

"Er, she doesn't seem to want to join in."

"Pull her up sharply with the leash and tell her firmly to stand."

Mr. Hamley tugged gently on Dotty's leash. "Come on, Dotty, stand!" he hissed.

Neil could see the other dog owners glancing sympathetically at Mr. Hamley, and he knew how awful his teacher must feel with all the attention.

But Dotty wouldn't move.

"Now, you must show her you mean it," Mr. Parker told Mr. Hamley. "Your voice is very important. Try imagining you are back in the classroom! A dog will only obey you if you speak with authority. Pull Dotty's leash again and tell her firmly and loudly to stand. It won't hurt her, and it will give her the jolt she needs to get her to pay attention to you."

Mr. Hamley tried again. "Dotty, *stand!*" His voice echoed around the barn and Neil winced. This was the Hamley he knew back at school!

Dotty stared at him in surprise and got to her feet.

"That's it! Good!" Bob said to him. Mr. Hamley flushed with pleasure and relief.

"And always praise your dog every time she does the right thing," Mr. Parker instructed the whole group. "Let's see you making a big fuss over your dogs now."

While everyone stooped to pat their dogs, Mr. Hamley led Dotty over to join the others on their circuit around the barn. "Good girl, Dotty," he said to her. "Good girl!"

For a while Dotty trotted quite happily alongside Mr. Hamley. While she wasn't actually walking to heel, she wasn't way in front of him, either, so Neil felt she was making progress.

"Now, we're going to get your dogs to sit," said Mr. Parker. "And when they do, give them lots of praise again."

Steve groaned and Neil smiled. Getting Ricky to sit was always a problem.

"Sit, Ricky!" Steve ordered firmly, pressing his free hand down on Ricky's rump.

Ricky wagged his tail and stayed standing.

"Sit!" Steve said, holding his hand out flat and moving it in a downward motion to try and show the Labrador what he meant.

Ricky immediately lay on the floor, his head on his front paws, and sighed.

Beside them, Mr. Hamley was having the same trouble with Dotty.

Dotty lay on the floor waiting to be tickled. Poor Mr. Hamley looked around desperately.

"Don't worry, she'll pick it up," Mr. Parker told him. "It might help if you show her more clearly what you want her to do. Here, let me show you."

Bob took Dotty's lead and made her stand beside him. "Sit, Dotty!" he said. He pressed her rump down firmly while pulling back on her leash. "Sit!"

Dotty sat.

"Good girl," Bob told her, giving her a treat from his pocket.

Dotty gobbled it down and sniffed around for more.

"Just keep at it patiently," he told Mr. Hamley, "and always try to reward her, either with a treat or by making a big fuss over her. After a while she'll sit on command and you can just reward her every now and then."

They practiced the sitting command once more. Honey was so obliging that Neil was able to relax. It gave him a chance to watch the others, and he was especially pleased to see Mr. Hamley finally get Dotty to sit. Was she responding at last?

"Now, let's try the 'stay and recall,'" Mr. Parker said, arranging the class in a long line. "I want you to tell your dogs to sit, then back away from them a few paces to the extent of their leashes and call them to you with a tug on the leash." He waited while everyone complained about being asked to do the impossible. "When they obey, give them lots of praise and fuss."

Honey didn't like Neil backing away from her. She tried at first to keep up with him, so he had to concentrate on making her sit and stay. Finally she got it right and he was able to look up and watch Dotty's progress.

Mr. Hamley did his best. As soon as he started to move back, though, Dotty got up and followed him.

"No, Dotty! *Stay!*" Mr. Hamley pleaded.

Dotty finally stayed. She watched her owner curiously, her head tilted to one side as he walked back a few paces, the leash at its full length.

"Come, Dotty!" shouted Mr. Hamley, tugging her leash. "Come!"

Dotty immediately bounded over to him, jumped up, and started licking his face.

"Down, Dotty!" Mr. Hamley whispered, trying to push her down. The dog just continued licking his face. Mr. Hamley tottered, trying to keep his balance as the young dog pressed her paws against him.

Mr. Parker came up behind and pushed Dotty down sharply. "*Down, Dotty!*" he commanded sternly.

Dotty sat down suddenly.

"Good girl," said Bob, patting her. Dotty pushed

her nose into his pocket, thinking she might get another treat.

"No, Dotty, that's greedy!" Mr. Hamley scolded her.

"That's OK," laughed Bob. "At least it shows you she's a quick learner when she wants to be!"

Steve turned to Neil. "She's even worse than Ricky," he marveled, a hint of admiration in his voice. "Mr. Hamley's your teacher, isn't he? Lucky you — he looks really soft!"

"Only with his dog," Neil whispered. "In school he can be a real nightmare."

As the lesson continued, Neil looked over at Dotty from time to time, but he saw little sign of improvement. She pulled on her leash, barking and trying to chase the other dogs. He felt sorry for Mr. Hamley, trying to control her. The teacher was probably very relieved when Mr. Parker announced a final circuit of the barn, walking their dogs to heel.

"Well, she got off to a bit of a bad start, but that's only to be expected at first," Bob Parker told Mr. Hamley at the close of the session. "Young dogs like Dotty can be very high-spirited — it's a bit like having a teenager around the house. But a couple more lessons and you'll see a big difference in her. And you might find it easier to control her if you use a choke chain. They're very good for preventing big strong dogs like Dotty from pulling ahead too much — but you must make sure that you put it on correctly."

Mr. Hamley nodded. "Thanks. I'll see about one tomorrow. Anything that helps me control Dotty is worth a try!"

Mr. Parker was addressing everyone now. "I want you all to practice the walking-to-heel and sit commands with your dogs. Just a few minutes a day will do. And remember that praise!"

"Bob's a marvelous trainer," Neil heard Mrs. Swinton say to Mr. Hamley. "He worked wonders with my sister's dog, you know, and she was awful — really disobedient and aggressive. But within a couple of months Bob had totally transformed her. It was wonderful."

Dotty was standing up now, pulling impatiently at her leash, eager to go.

"Wait a minute, Dotty!" said Mr. Hamley. Dotty barked loudly and looked over at the door. Then she tore off, catching her owner off guard and tugging the leash out of his hand.

"Oh, no! Dotty! Come back!" he shouted, giving chase as the Dalmatian bolted from the barn.

Other dogs barked and tried to follow. They wanted to join in the fun, too. The noise was deafening as the owners struggled to hang on to their animals.

Neil quickly gave Honey back to her owner and joined his father as he went after Dotty. They were just in time to see the Dalmatian disappearing toward the Parkers' backyard with Mr. Hamley chasing after her. Suddenly she stopped in the middle of the lawn. To relieve herself.

"Maybe we can catch her now!" laughed Mr. Parker, watching the dog squatting on his newly mowed grass.

Neil grinned. Dotty was such a character!

"Dotty! You naughty girl!" Mr. Hamley roared, running over to her. "Come here!" As he lunged for the leash, Dotty promptly turned and ran between his legs. He lost his balance and fell just a bit too close to the mess Dotty had deposited on the grass. Neil thought this was perhaps not the time to remind him of the poop-scoop rule.

A gale of laughter from the direction of the barn told Neil that the other dog owners had come outside to see what was happening. Now they stood enjoying the joke, thanking their lucky stars that Dotty wasn't their dog.

Dotty, meanwhile, was heading toward the boarding kennels. Neil looked at his father. His lips twitching, Mr. Parker turned and caught Neil's eye. "Whatever you do, don't laugh," he whispered, his own eyes twinkling. "The poor man feels awful enough already."

Neil understood.

"I'll get her, sir," he called to Mr. Hamley, who was staring in dismay at his dirty jacket.

Neil soon found Dotty, standing outside the pen of

Jed, the Great Dane. The two dogs were showing great interest in each other, so Neil sneaked up behind Dotty and quickly grabbed her leash.

Instantly she tried to pull away.

"Oh no you don't!" Neil told her, holding the leash firmly.

"Well done, Neil!" said his father, coming up beside him.

Mr. Hamley was trailing behind, looking weary and flustered. His normally immaculate dark hair was rumpled and his cheeks flushed. He'd taken his jacket off and was carrying it over his arm. Once he saw Dotty had been caught, he strode over.

"Thank you," he said stiffly. "I'll take her now." He almost snatched Dotty's leash out of Neil's hand and walked away.

"I'll see you all next week," Mr. Parker said loudly for the benefit of Mr. Hamley's departing back. "And remember there's also a class on Sunday morning at ten-thirty if you'd like to come along."

"I don't think we'll be coming again," said Mr. Hamley, turning back briefly. "It's obvious that Dotty is untrainable and I don't intend to be a further source of amusement for anyone."

"But, sir . . ." Neil began.

"Come on, Dotty!" he ordered, tugging her leash.

Neil watched them go with a sinking heart.

CHAPTER SIX

"**D**o you think Mr. Hamley meant it about not bringing Dotty again?" Neil asked his father as they ate breakfast the next morning.

Mr. Parker chewed his toast thoughtfully.

"I think he was more embarrassed than anything else," he replied. "Maybe he'll change his mind when he's calmed down a bit."

Neil hoped so. He finished his breakfast and grabbed a few doggy treats before hurrying over to see Sandy. He was sure he knew how to get Sandy to trust him. He wanted to try, anyway.

The other two rescued dogs started barking excitedly as Neil opened the door of the center and stepped inside. He stopped to say a quick hello to them both as he passed.

As usual, Sandy retreated to the far wall when Neil approached.

"Hey, come on, boy. No one's going to hurt you," Neil said gently. He held up a treat and pushed it through the wire. "Here you are."

Once Neil moved away from the fence, Sandy came forward and snatched up the food. Then he looked guardedly over at Neil.

"I'll come back and see you later, feller," Neil told him. He knew this was going to be a long process. If he tried to rush it he would make the dog even more nervous.

Neil glanced at his watch. There was just enough time to see Buttons as well.

The sad little dog showed no improvement, though. She lay in the corner of her kennel and made no effort to come and get the snack he offered.

Neil wished he could stay at home and spend some time with both dogs. Especially today. He was dreading facing Mr. Hamley after Dotty's disastrous lesson the previous evening. Mr. Hamley was bound to be in a foul mood.

He heard Emily shout as he ran back across the courtyard.

"Neil! Chris is here!"

"Coming!" Neil grabbed his bike and wheeled it out through the side gate. Chris was waiting for him in the driveway.

"So how did the lesson go with Dotty last night?" he asked eagerly.

Neil grimaced and told him all about it. "I'm dreading this morning. I bet my name's mud with Hamley," he said.

Mr. Hamley didn't actually say anything to Neil. In fact he wasn't his normal self at all. He was very quiet and preoccupied all day.

"Well, Smiler's in a weird mood, isn't he?" Hasheem said as they walked out of the classroom. "I made two jokes and he didn't even notice. I wonder what's up with him."

Neil shrugged. "Maybe he's got something on his mind." It wasn't hard to guess what.

Mr. Hamley must be pretty upset about Dotty's behavior. Then why couldn't he see that giving up training classes was the worst thing he could do?

To Neil's disappointment, there was no sign of the Dalmatian in Sunday's class.

"Couldn't you call him and talk him into giving Dotty another chance?" Neil asked his father when the last of the dogs had left. "If you told him lots of dogs behaved worse than Dotty when they first came, he might not feel so bad."

Mr. Parker sighed. "You know I can't interfere like

that. It's up to Mr. Hamley whether he brings his dog to the class or not."

Just then Carole Parker shouted across the courtyard to the barn.

"Bob! Paul Hamley's on the phone!"

"Maybe he's changed his mind after all," said Neil eagerly.

"Maybe," replied his father, striding over to the office.

Neil had just finished tidying up the barn when Mr. Parker came back ten minutes later.

"The Hamleys have decided to bring Dotty here for a bit," he told Neil.

"Here?" Neil said, surprised.

"Yes. I got the impression they were both at the end of their tethers with Dotty. Rachel Hamley's baby is due soon and she just can't cope with such a boisterous dog. They want to board Dotty here for the time being."

"Until the baby's born?"

"Until they find another home for her."

"What? But if they kept bringing her to lessons she'd be fine," Neil persisted. Dotty was such a lovely dog. It didn't seem fair that she had to go to another home. It would be terrible for her.

Bob Parker watched his son's face cloud over with concern and disappointment. He understood exactly Neil's sense of frustration. "I could only train Dotty if

Mr. Hamley was prepared to learn how to handle her, Neil. But he's just too soft with her and a bit nervous. A big dog like that needs firmness and confidence."

Neil nodded, not trusting himself to say anything.

"Well, I'll go and get a pen ready. She'll be arriving later today."

Neil watched his father walk over to the kennel blocks. Poor Dotty! He just hoped that Mr. Hamley and his wife would miss her so much they'd come and get her after a day or two.

He couldn't imagine having to give away his dog to some stranger. Supposing it was Sam. No — the thought was too terrible. Whatever happened, he'd make sure he gave the Dalmatian lots of love and attention while she was here.

Mr. Hamley arrived with Dotty at three o'clock. Neil and Emily followed their father to the kennels to show Mr. Hamley where Dotty would be staying. Neil could see he was very distressed, but trying hard not to show it.

"Now, you . . . you be a good girl, Dotty," he said gently, his voice wavering. He stroked her head, turning his face away from them while he led her into the pen. "I'll come and see you soon."

He stood up and blew his nose noisily into his handkerchief.

"Sorry — bit of a cold. I'm very grateful to you for

taking Dotty at such short notice. I'm not sure how long it will take me to find her a suitable home, so she could be here a while."

"Don't worry, she'll be fine with us," Mr. Parker assured him. "I'll use my contacts, too, if you like. Dotty's a lovely dog, even if she is a bit unruly. It shouldn't be too difficult to find somebody to take her on."

"Thank you. I'd appreciate that," Mr. Hamley told him.

"Maybe you could take Dotty back when Mrs. Hamley's had the baby?" Neil said hopefully.

His teacher shook his head sadly. "We wish we could keep Dotty, Neil. Rachel and I think the world of her. But I'm afraid Dotty's just too unmanageable to have in the same house as a newborn baby. It's an impossible situation."

And with one final glance at Dotty, Mr. Hamley walked away.

Dotty watched him go, pressing her muzzle to the wire and whining softly.

"Poor Dotty!" Emily said. "And poor Mr. Hamley. He seems so sad about leaving her here. Can't we do something, Dad?"

Mr. Parker shrugged. "I don't see what. After all, it's their decision. While I think it's a shame for Dotty, they have to think of their baby first. And who knows? Dotty might well be happier with someone who can manage her better."

Neil knew his dad was right but it didn't make him feel any better.

Then he had an idea. There could be a way of changing his teacher's mind. If his father agreed, it was worth a try.

"Couldn't we train Dotty before Mr. Hamley finds her somewhere to go?" Neil suggested. "Then he wouldn't need to get rid of her."

His father shook his head. "We can't work with Dotty without Mr. Hamley knowing, Neil. It wouldn't be right. She's still his dog."

"But it's Dotty's only chance now," Neil pleaded. "And I'm sure Mr. Hamley won't mind. He did want her trained, after all."

"Well . . ." His father hesitated. "I suppose it couldn't hurt . . ."

"Come on, Dad. We can give it a try at least," begged Emily. "Otherwise poor Dotty will be sold. And anyway, she'll still be terrible for her new owners and then they might get rid of her, too."

"Point taken. OK, I'll include Dotty in my training classes and see how she does," Mr. Parker agreed. "And you can give her some extra practice in the evenings. But don't expect it to be easy."

Neil and Emily both grinned.

It would be tough, they knew, but it would be worth it — for Dotty's sake!

The next day, Emily's sponsor forms came from the SPCA. Carole Parker helped her fill them in sitting at the kitchen table, while Neil helped Sarah draw a very colorful picture of Sam.

"We'll keep one form in the office," said Carole. "I'm sure some of our regulars will sponsor Sam." Most of the customers who used King Street Kennels usually visited the office at some point, either to collect their dogs, pay their bill, or arrange for their pets to stay.

"Thanks, Mom. Let's take one to school, too, Neil," Emily said. "Some of the kids will sponsor us. And the teachers."

"We could go down to Mrs. Smedley's after school

and ask her if we can leave one there," said Neil. "Lots of people stop in every day."

Bob Parker came in from his morning rounds, looking rather worried.

"How's Dotty?" Neil asked anxiously. He hoped she wasn't moping. He was planning to go and see her, and Sandy and Buttons, before he went to school. His visiting list was getting longer every day, it seemed.

"She's settled down quite well," his father told him. "It's Buttons I'm worried about. She's still not eating very much."

"Maybe Buttons wants something to cuddle up to," suggested Sarah. "Cuddling my teddy bear always makes me feel better."

"Get real, Squirt," scoffed Emily. "As if Buttons wants a teddy bear!"

"Hang on. Sarah's right. Buttons probably would like something to comfort her," their father said thoughtfully. "Not a teddy bear, though. Something belonging to Mr. or Mrs. Timms that she can lie on in her basket. An item of clothing, perhaps — that sometimes does the trick."

"I've got their neighbors' phone number," said Mrs. Parker. "I'll call them and see if they've got any suggestions. They might even have a spare key to the house."

*   *   *

When Neil arrived home from school later that day, his mother told him she'd managed to contact Mrs. Timms' neighbor.

"His name is Geoff Wilkins, and he sounds really nice," she told them. "He's got an old gardening sweater that Mrs. Timms left there recently when she stopped by for a cup of coffee, and he's bringing it over. He thought Buttons might cheer up if she sees a familiar face, so he's going to give her the sweater himself."

"Great!" said Neil. "Hope it works."

"So do I. I don't know what else we can do."

Half an hour later, a blue car pulled up in the drive and a tall, broad man with red cheeks got out, holding a green sweater. Neil ran to open the door, telling Sarah to get their mother.

"Hello there! Are you one of the Parker children?" the man asked cheerfully. "Could you tell your mother that Geoff Wilkins is here?"

"I'm Neil Parker. Mom'll be out in a minute, Mr. Wilkins," Neil said politely.

His mother came out of the side gate.

"Mr. Wilkins? How kind of you to come."

"Happy to help," said Mr. Wilkins. "Poor old Buttons! Joe and Alice would be very upset if they knew how distressed she was."

He followed Mrs. Parker to where Buttons was lying in her pen, her eyes sad and anxious.

"Oh, dear!" said Mr. Wilkins. "Just look at her!"

At the sound of his voice, Buttons pricked her ears and lifted her head.

"Hey, girl, it's me!" Mr. Wilkins said as Carole pulled open the pen door. "And just look what I've brought for you!"

He stepped inside and knelt down, the green sweater draped over his knee.

Buttons ran over and jumped up to him eagerly, licking his face. Then she sniffed at the sweater. The change in her was remarkable. She nuzzled the sweater ecstatically, whining and barking.

Geoff walked over to Buttons' basket and arranged the sweater inside it.

Buttons ran over. She sniffed at the sweater again, pawed it into place and then lay down on it. The listless look had disappeared from her face.

"Happy now, girl?" he asked, stroking her gently.

"Just look at that!" Mrs. Parker smiled. "It seems to have done the trick. Thank you so much, Mr. Wilkins. Perhaps if we leave her by herself for a while she might even eat her dinner."

They all walked out of the pen and Mrs. Parker closed it behind them.

"Would you mind if I popped in to see Buttons again, before Joe and Alice return?" Mr. Wilkins asked as they returned to the house. "I'm very fond of her, you know. In fact, I would have taken her in myself if I wasn't out all day at work."

"Please come and visit her anytime you like," said Mrs. Parker.

"I will then. Thank you!" Mr. Wilkins said, waving as he got into his car.

"Well, hopefully that's one problem solved," said Neil's mom as they watched Mr. Wilkins drive off.

A quick check on Buttons after dinner showed Neil that the little dog was indeed her old self again. She was running around her exercise pen, tossing and chasing an old rubber bone that her owners had left with her. She ran to the fence, barking, when she saw Neil, and wagged her tail happily.

"Attagirl, Buttons. You've really cheered up now,

haven't you?" Neil said, crouching down and poking his fingers through the fence to be licked.

"Sure has!" said his father, behind him. "Eaten all her dinner, too."

"Great!" said Neil. "I'm just going to say good night to Dotty."

"Be quick," added his father. "I'll be locking up in five minutes."

The Dalmatian trotted over as Neil approached her pen. She nuzzled his fingers and pawed at the chain-link fence, asking to be let out.

"Oh, Dotty," he said, stroking her head. "I'd love to take you home. But you'll have to be patient. It's not going to be quite so easy getting your problem fixed!"

CHAPTER SEVEN

Neil took Dotty through her paces at his father's obedience class on Wednesday, and then gave her extra lessons by himself every night. He took Sam with him to these sessions, to set an example for Dotty and help her to socialize sensibly with another dog. To his delight, the two dogs soon became good friends and Dotty enjoyed copying Sam as Neil put them through the basic exercises.

It was tiring work.

It meant patiently repeating and repeating simple commands until Dotty did what he wanted, and always rewarding and praising her when she got it right.

He couldn't overlook his other chores and homework, either.

Emily sometimes kept them company, admiring Neil's calm determination and Dotty's willingness to please him. Neil never got angry with her.

By Sunday morning Dotty was beginning to show signs of real improvement.

"What do you think, Dad?" Neil asked before lunch that day. He had just demonstrated how Dotty would sit on command and come when he called her.

Mr. Parker smiled down at the dog nosing in Neil's pocket, looking for a treat. "She's doing great. And so are you, Neil. Don't tire yourself out, though."

"Don't worry. We're going to train Sam for the show now." Neil grinned as his father rolled his eyes. "Can I take Dotty over, too? She learns a lot from watching Sam at work."

"That's fine. Just don't let her run loose, will you?"

"I won't!" Neil clipped a strong leash to her collar. "Come on, Dotty! Let's go!"

Emily was already in the field with Sam, setting out the Agility course as before. She looked up and smiled when she heard Dotty barking and came over to pat her. Sam joined them, wagging his tail happily at Dotty.

How different the two dogs were, thought Neil. Dotty was taller and sleeker than Sam with her smooth, short fur and boisterous, playful personality. Sam was an older dog, steady and reliable, with a long, glossy coat. He might have been a little jeal-

ous at first of all the attention Dotty was getting from Neil, but he had soon gotten over it.

Neil handed Dotty's leash to his sister. "Here, you hang on to her while I put Sam through his paces."

Emily led the Dalmatian away and they sat together in the grass to watch as Sam ran around the course, jumping over the hurdles, through a tire, weaving in and out of posts, and running up and down planks. He particularly loved the tunnel, barking excitedly as he ran through. He seemed to know exactly what to do and completed the makeshift course in no time.

"Terrific!" Emily clapped her hands enthusiastically. "Well done, Sam!"

Dotty barked and stood up, looking eagerly at the course.

"I think Dotty wants to try," called Emily. "Shall we let her?"

Neil looked at the Dalmatian struggling to come across and join him.

"OK, give her a try, but keep her on the leash, Em," Neil agreed. "Let's see what she can do!"

As soon as they reached the first jump, Dotty sailed over it in one graceful leap.

"Wow! Look at that!" exclaimed Emily, running hard to keep up. "Dotty's a natural!"

Neil watched as the Dalmatian raced through the course. She had to run around some of the obstacles because Emily had her leash in a firm grip, but Dotty cleared every jump. Sam stood watching her, barking his approval.

"Neil, I've got a brilliant idea!" Emily said excitedly.

Neil groaned. Emily's brilliant ideas often meant trouble. "I don't think I want to hear this, do I?"

"Yes, you do. Listen. Why don't we train Dotty and enter her in the show as well as Sam?"

"Why?"

"If she does well," his sister continued, "Mr. and Mrs. Hamley will be able to see how well trained she is, and they'll be so proud, they're bound to want to keep her. What do you think?"

Neil shook his head. "We can't do that! Dotty

would never be good enough in time. The show is next week."

"She would if we worked with her every night. And it might be Dotty's only chance to go back home," Emily pointed out.

Neil thought about it. It wouldn't be too difficult for him to enter two dogs for the competition — he and Emily could share the extra registration fee — and he remembered only too well Dotty's sad face and pitiful whining when Mr. Hamley had walked away after his visit yesterday. If there was a chance of helping her go back home again, Neil had to take it.

"OK," he decided. "But we'll have to ask Dad. He may not agree."

"There's only one way to find out. Let's take the dogs back and ask him."

They found their father in his office, frowning over some papers. He listened as Neil and Emily eagerly outlined their plan. Then he shook his head.

"Sorry, kids, it's a nice idea, but it wouldn't work," he said. "Dotty isn't our dog. We would need to get Mr. Hamley's permission before entering her in a show. And what if she runs off? She'd be the responsibility of King Street Kennels and it wouldn't look very good for us if she behaved badly."

"I'll train her to manage it," Neil insisted. "I can do it."

"I know you'll try, Neil. You've worked wonders with Sam. But Dotty's different. She's not a young puppy like Sam was — she's much harder to train. It's too risky. Sorry, but I have to say no."

"But, Dad . . ."

"I'm sorry, Neil. Come on, take Dotty back to her pen, please. She could probably do with a drink of water and a rest now."

Neil and Emily turned away, disappointed.

"Well, I guess that's it," said Emily as they walked away. "Dad sounded pretty serious."

"Never mind, we'll still keep working with you, Dotty," Neil said, stroking her. "We'll show your owners what you can do, eh?"

"If they don't sell her first," Emily reminded him. "I don't think they'll have any trouble selling such a beautiful Dalmatian. Do you think Mr. Hamley's advertised her yet?"

Neil hadn't thought of that. Emily was right. Dotty would be a prize catch for the right kind of owner. "I think he'd tell Dad if he had. Besides, people would have to come to the kennels to see her, wouldn't they?"

"Oh, yes. I hadn't thought of that." Emily nodded. "C'mon, I'll take Sam back while you take care of Dotty."

After Neil had settled Dotty in her kennel, he hurried over to the rescue center to look in on Sandy.

Neil had been taking him a biscuit every day and

to his delight the dog had started to respond. He no longer growled when he saw Neil, although he still watched warily from the corner of the pen and wouldn't touch anything Neil left until he had moved away.

Today, Sandy was lying in his basket. He sat up and silently watched Neil approach, but made no other attempt to move.

"Hello, Sandy," Neil said softly, pleased with Sandy's response. If he could just get him to trust people again, there might be a chance of finding him a good home.

After school the next day, Neil and Emily biked down into Compton to the magazine store to see how many sponsors had signed their form. It had been displayed for over a week now and they were hoping for a good response.

"Hi, Neil, Emily," said Tom cheerily as they walked in. Tom was Mrs. Smedley's son and a student at college. He helped out at the store whenever he could. "What can I get for you?"

"We wondered if anyone had signed our sponsor form," Neil told him.

"I'll say they have. Just look at this!" Tom grinned and showed them the form. It was almost full. "Bring another form down and I bet we'll get that filled up, too, before the show."

"Actually," Emily said with a straight face, pulling

a sponsor form from her pocket and flattening it out on the counter, "I just happen to have one on me."

Tom laughed aloud and Neil smiled. Trust Emily to come prepared!

They stopped by Chris's house on the way home. He answered his front door wearing a very muddy soccer uniform that had once been black-and-white.

Neil looked him up and down with a raised eyebrow.

"You up for a training session with Sam?" he asked his friend. "You look as if Dotty's been walking all over you!"

"Funny!" Chris replied dryly. "Let me get changed first. I just got back from soccer practice."

"I'd never have guessed!"

Half an hour later they were all in the field with Sam. As usual, the smart dog completed the Agility course with flying colors, still enjoying it all hugely despite the number of times he had been through it.

"Wow! Look at him go!" Chris yelled, whooping with delight.

"Way to go, Sam!" Neil said, making a big fuss over him.

"I bet he's the fastest dog in the show!" said Chris. "And the smartest!"

"'Course he is, aren't you, Sam?" said Emily. Sam barked his agreement and they all laughed.

"How's Dotty's training coming along?" asked Chris.

"She sits and comes on command now," Neil told him proudly. "Let's take Sam back and I'll show you."

Dotty was in her outside run. She came bounding in when she saw Chris and Neil enter the pen. She barked excitedly, raced over to them, and went to jump up at them.

"No, Dotty. Sit!" Neil told her firmly.

Dotty sat obediently, but quivered with excitement and wagged her tail furiously. It was hard for Neil not to laugh, she looked so comical.

Chris was not so restrained. "She'll fall over in a minute!" he laughed.

"Good girl," Neil said, patting her. "Now, stay!"

Dotty sat still, not moving a muscle, but watching Neil intently as he backed away from her — alert for his next signal.

"Come, Dotty! Here, girl!"

Dotty charged over to sit at his feet, waiting to be praised.

Chris looked really impressed. "I can hardly believe she's the same dog," he said. "Old Smiler's going to be surprised."

Neil told his friend how he and Emily had wanted to put Dotty in the show as well as Sam. "Dad said we can't. He's worried Dotty might run off or something."

"That's a real shame," said Chris. "Any chance he might change his mind?"

"Not a hope," Neil told him. "When Dad says no, he means it."

After Chris had gone home, Neil made his regular trip to see Sandy. To his surprise, Sandy jumped out of his basket and ran over to the fence, barking and wagging his tail. Neil was delighted.

"Sandy! Hey there, feller! You look pleased to see me."

Sandy cocked his head expectantly at Neil.

"So, you want a treat?" Neil asked, reaching in his pocket.

"Hold on, let's go into the pen to give him that. I'd like to see how he reacts."

Neil turned around to see his father standing by him.

"Dad! I didn't know you were here."

"I was cleaning out one of the other pens when I heard you come in," said Mr. Parker. He opened Sandy's pen. "Now make sure you go in quietly and slowly," he told Neil.

Sandy backed away a little and watched them warily as Neil stepped inside.

"Come on, Sandy. Good boy." Neil held out a biscuit and put it on the floor by his feet.

Sandy hesitated for a moment before running over and snatching it up. He came over to Neil and nudged his hand.

"Want some more, do you?" Neil laughed softly, reaching out to stroke Sandy's head.

Sandy flinched and stiffened for a moment, then started to lick Neil's hand.

"Look, Dad. He trusts me!" Neil said, overjoyed. "He isn't growling anymore."

"So I see," said Mr. Parker. "You've done a good job, Neil. He's nowhere near as receptive to Kate. And you know how good she is with the dogs."

As they left the center, Neil told his father how he'd been to see Sandy every day, giving him treats and gradually building up his trust. "I just wanted him to know that not everyone is going to mistreat him," he said.

"And you've succeeded," his father said. "Well done! I thought Sandy was settling down a bit, but I didn't realize it was thanks so much to your efforts. I had a call this morning from someone looking for a new dog but I didn't think Sandy would be right for them. A family over in Padsham. They have a son your age. I'm thinking now that maybe I can help them after all."

"Sandy might have a new home?" Neil was pleased that this was one story that was going to have a quick, happy ending. "Great!"

"You've certainly got your dad's way with dogs, Neil," said Carole Parker that evening as they prepared to eat their meal.

"I know," Emily agreed. "He can get them to do anything. I bet he could train Dotty to do the Agility course in no time." She cast a sly glance at her father who had just entered the kitchen with a printed leaflet in his hand.

"What's this? You're putting Dotty in the show?" her mother asked.

Bob Parker took his time before answering.

"Is there some problem, Bob?" asked Carole, suspecting something was wrong.

"I've found the entry form at last replied heavily, looking apologetical

"What's the matter, Dad?" asked ~~Neil,~~ dread creeping over him.

"Well, the last date for registration forms and fees is the day after tomorrow. That's all right — I know the secretary of the show and I can drop it off at his house. The problem is, all dogs have to be registered with the Kennel Club before they can enter."

He waited for his news to sink in.

"Kennel Club?" asked Neil, not understanding. "But Sam's a rescued dog, not a pedigree."

"It doesn't matter. He has to have a Kennel Club name and a number before he can enter an Agility contest. It's the rule, Neil."

"Does that mean he'll never be able to compete?" Emily asked.

"No. We can get him registered. But it will take time, and we don't have long enough before this county show. He'll have to wait until the next one. I'm sorry, son."

"Poor Sam," said Sarah. "Will Fudge have to have a number, too?"

"No, dear," her mother reassured her quietly. "Fudge is going to be in a different competition."

Neil stared miserably at the kitchen table, not really listening. All his hopes were squashed. All Sam's training for nothing.

"I suppose we'll have to cancel the sponsorship and everything," said Emily.

An atmosphere of gloom settled over them all.

"Well, maybe not," said Mr. Parker slowly. "I've been thinking about your idea of putting Dotty in the Agility competition, Emily, and I think it might be possible after all."

"Dad, that's great!" Emily squealed.

Neil looked across at his father, wondering.

"Your idea got me thinking, so I took the liberty of asking Paul Hamley to send over copies of her registration forms and pedigree. It did occur to me that she might not be old enough to compete." He turned to the others to explain. "Dogs have to be at least eighteen months old to take part in Agility competitions — the course is too demanding for younger dogs. Anyway, it turns out Dotty is just eighteen months old and she *is* registered with the Kennel Club, so she qualifies on both counts."

"Yeah! Terrific!" yelled Emily, who had always thought her idea was great.

"But what about the Hamleys, Dad?" Neil asked. He couldn't believe the problem could be solved so simply.

"Well, they did take some convincing, I admit," replied his father, "but Paul has given his permission on the understanding that King Street Kennels takes full responsibility for the whole thing — and pays the fee, of course!"

They all laughed. But Neil didn't know what to think. He was desperately disappointed about Sam being disqualified, but this new development meant that Dotty might get a chance to be reunited with the Hamleys. And Neil would still get to take part in his first Agility competition — something he had really been looking forward to.

"You've worked wonders with Sandy, Neil," Mr. Parker said. "I'm impressed."

Neil went slightly red.

"I think you deserve a chance to work with Dotty. And I think it's just the kind of character reference Dotty needs, too, if the Hamleys are to give her a second chance."

"You mean it, Dad?" Neil asked. "We can really enter Dotty in the show?"

Their father nodded. "On the condition that her training continues under my supervision and according to my instructions. OK?"

"OK, Dad," Neil promised. Getting Dotty trained was too important to mess up. He was going to do everything properly and show Mr. and Mrs. Hamley just what an obedient dog Dotty could be. "So where's this entry form?"

CHAPTER EIGHT

Neil's first job as soon as he and Emily arrived home from school the next day was to fill in Sam's registration form for the Kennel Club. He had to think of three names for him, so that the Kennel Club could choose one not already in use. Although Emily begged him, he refused to let her see what he had written.

The second job was to start Dotty's training. Sam and Emily came along as well.

Dotty watched, barking encouragement as Sam ran around the course first.

"She's very excited! Look!" Emily said.

Neil called Sam over and commanded him to lie down. Then he took Dotty to the starting point and released her.

As soon as she was off her leash, the Dalmatian ignored the jumps and sprinted across the field, bounding playfully in the long grass and barking at Sam. Emily put up a hand to show Sam he was to stay.

Neil felt a stab of fear as he saw Dotty running around so wildly. He called her back.

She did not respond the first time, but at the second command she obediently trotted over to him.

"Good girl!" he praised her with considerable relief. He took her back to the start of the course.

"Go, Dotty! Go!" he shouted.

He ran alongside her, getting her to stop at every obstacle so he could show her what to do. Dotty had no trouble with the jumps but was confused by the planks — the "dog walk" as they were called — and kept jumping off them. Neil made sure they finished the course with a jump so he could praise her lavishly.

Emily, however, looked anxious. For the first time she was having doubts about what they were doing. "Do you think you'll get her trained in time? The show's on Saturday."

"I think so. If I work with her every night this week, she should pick it up. She's got to."

"I just hope Mr. Hamley doesn't come to visit while we're practicing," Emily said as she took Dotty back to her pen. "She'd forget what she was doing."

"He usually comes after dinner, Em. So if we keep working with Dotty right after school, we should be OK."

"How's Dotty?" asked Carole Parker on Thursday evening, as she worked at the computer. Neil and Emily were in the office, helping their mother file paperwork. Sarah was building a paper clip mountain.

"We had to get Sam to go along the dog walk three times first," said Neil, "and I went along it myself before Dotty got the hang of what to do. I'm just glad I didn't have to show her how to jump through the tire!"

"She kept jumping off too soon," Emily explained.

"Huh! Climbing isn't hard. Fudge can do that," Sarah piped up. "He climbs up his ladder and he goes in and out of his tubes. He'd come in first in any Agility course."

"I'm sure he would, Sarah," said Carole. "But training Dotty is a bit special. It sounds to me as if you are both doing extremely well." She smiled over at them. "Keep it up, kids."

Neil and Emily grinned. A little encouragement helped a lot.

"But what if the Hamleys don't come to the show?" Emily asked suddenly. "What do we do then?"

"They'll be there," her mother assured her. She hit a button on the computer keyboard. The nearby printer buzzed into life and began to churn out a copy of her document. "Rachel Hamley told me she wants to watch a friend in one of the horse-riding events."

"So they're bound to come and watch the Agility

competition, aren't they?" said Neil. "Especially after Mr. Hamley's sponsored our entry."

"He has?" said Mrs. Parker, wide-eyed with surprise.

"I just hope Dotty doesn't let us down," said Emily.

"So do I," said Neil. He didn't want to think how angry his teacher would be if Dotty misbehaved and their whole plan backfired.

Chris came over after dinner for a game of soccer.

"Let's get Dotty to join in, too," said Neil. "She's been working really hard. I'm sure she'd enjoy some fun."

Dotty wasn't sure what to do at first, but she ran around enthusiastically, trying to get the ball, and tangling herself in everyone's legs. It was a trick Sam soon learned, too. He took fiendish delight in tripping them up. No one was spared.

Tired of being outsmarted by dogs, Chris cheated by picking up the ball and running with it toward the goal.

"Sam!" Neil shouted. "Tackle the ball!"

The Border collie ran like a rocket in front of Chris, making him trip and drop the ball.

Chris tried to call "Foul!" but he was laughing too hard.

Sam stole the ball away from him, started to push it over to Neil, who was yelling encouragement, but

lost it to Emily, who kicked it away. The ball went shooting over the field toward Dotty, with Sam in hot pursuit.

Both dogs raced after the ball. Dotty had a longer stride than Sam, though, and reached it first. Determined not to let Sam steal it, she picked it up in her mouth and ran back triumphantly with it to Neil, dropping it at his feet.

Then she wagged her tail, looking very pleased with herself, as if to say, "How about a reward?"

Emily, Chris, and Neil collapsed in the grass, laughing and gasping.

"Well, that's one way of getting the ball!" Neil said when he could speak at last.

"I don't think Dotty is cut out for soccer!" laughed

Chris, still trying to get his breath back. "She doesn't appreciate the finer points of the rules, does she, Sam?"

"Look who's talking!" scoffed Neil, and the game degenerated into a wrestling match, involving them all.

"Do you think she's ready, Neil?" asked Emily on Friday evening. They'd set off with Dotty for her last training lesson in the field.

"Well, we won't be able to tell until the real thing," Neil told her. "She's been doing well on our homemade course, but who knows what she'll do with all those people watching and a different course to follow."

Emily watched anxiously as Neil took Dotty around the course once more. The Dalmatian seemed to have no trouble now with any of the obstacles.

"She's done it! She's done it!" Emily clapped excitedly as Dotty completed her first clear round in excellent time.

"Good girl, Dotty! I knew you could do it." Neil beamed with pleasure as he hugged the Dalmatian.

Dotty licked him happily.

He looked up to see his dad and Kate standing at the gate, watching.

"What do you think, Dad?" Neil called over to his father.

"Terrific. Both of you! All of you!"

Neil and Emily grinned. Sam wagged his tail.

"I'll just take her through it one more time," said Neil.

To his immense relief and satisfaction, Dotty completed another clear round, to enthusiastic applause from her small audience.

"She's so good. Any chance she might win?" Emily asked.

"It depends a lot on what it's like tomorrow and the other competitors. I just want her to get around without too many penalties — or being eliminated," Neil told her. "That's what she's sponsored to do and that will show Mr. and Mrs. Hamley that she can be really obedient."

Neil and Emily crossed their fingers. The rest was up to Dotty now.

When they returned to the kennels, they found Mr. and Mrs. Timms had arrived to pick up Buttons. The little dog had settled down really well but she was overjoyed to see her owners again. She bounded over to them, wagging her tail and whimpering with excitement.

"Hello, Buttons! We've really missed you." Alice Timms smiled as the little dog jumped up at her, licked her excitedly, and then jumped up at Joe Timms.

"Look how pleased she is to see us!" said Mr. Timms as they both patted their happy little dog.

They were both surprised to see the old sweater in

her basket until Mr. Parker explained why it was there.

"We're really grateful to you for looking after her so well," said Mrs. Timms.

It was great to see Buttons so happy again. Neil gave her a big good-bye hug before helping Joe and Alice put the little dog and her basket into the back of their car. He was very glad everything had worked out so well.

Looking up as he walked back into the house, Neil saw his mother watching from the window. He could tell by the expression on her face that something was wrong.

"What's up, Mom?" he asked anxiously as he walked inside.

"Mr. Hamley's just called," she said. "I'm afraid he's found a new owner for Dotty. It's an old college friend of his who lives in London. He's bringing him to see her on Sunday."

Neil looked at her in dismay. *In London? That's miles away*, he thought. He'd never see Dotty again.

Everything hinged on the show, now. It was the only chance he had to prove to his teacher that Dotty was worth keeping.

CHAPTER NINE

"Just look at all these people! Where have they all come from?" said Emily, as they walked through the gates into the already crowded fairgrounds.

They had come early, so that Neil could report to the Agility ring in order to walk the course with the other competitors before the main crowds arrived.

It was a fine morning, promising to be a good day for the show.

Scores of people were setting up booths and attractions, or delivering their livestock for judging later in the day. There was even a group of country dancers going through their routine.

"The county show is always popular," said Mr. Parker. "It's not just local people who attend. They come from miles around, especially for the horse-riding events."

"I hope Fudge doesn't mind being kept awake," said Sarah, carrying his cage carefully in front of her with both hands.

Now that he was here, Neil was feeling decidedly nervous. Hundreds of butterflies were flying in his stomach.

"I hope we don't meet the Hamleys before our dog event starts," said Neil. "They might upset Dotty."

"Don't worry," his dad reassured him. "I know they're only coming for a short time today. The equestrian event they want to see isn't until late

morning. I doubt Rachel will want to walk around too much in her condition."

"I'm glad I'm looking after Sam," said Emily, glancing at the Border collie walking obediently by her side. "Dotty looks like she's going to run off any minute."

"I'll have to leave Dotty with you, Dad, while I walk the course," Neil pointed out.

"I think I can manage that," said his father, smiling.

Dotty was so excited by all the people and noise that she was pulling on her leash, eager to go off and explore.

Neil brought her to heel firmly.

The Dalmatian slowed her pace and walked quietly beside him.

"Good girl!" said Neil.

Mr. Parker glanced at his watch. "We'd better get over to the ring."

"I'll take Sarah to enter Fudge in the Cleverest Pet competition," said Mrs. Parker. "It's due to start soon in the big tent."

"Right. We'll join you as soon as we can," her husband said. "Good luck, Sarah!"

"Yeah, good luck, Squirt!" Neil and Emily waved as their mother and sister hurried toward the tent.

They turned a corner at the end of the display booths, and Neil's heart sank with dismay.

Part of the fairgrounds had been fenced off for the Agility course and Neil could see immediately that it was going to be a lot tougher than their homely arrangements of bits and pieces in the field. For a start the colors leaped out. Several items had large yellow squares on them. Contact points, he remembered. They hadn't used them at home. Too late to worry about them now.

The referee was walking toward them.

He checked Dotty's details on his list. In view of Neil's age and Dotty's inexperience, he entered them in the Junior category.

This was good in one respect — the course was simpler and they had a longer time limit — but it worked against them in another. The Junior event was open to anyone twelve years old and under, whether they were new to the competition or not.

Neil and Dotty could find themselves competing against a handler and dog with many competitions — and prizes — to their credit already. It was not a comforting thought.

While Emily and his father waited with the dogs, Neil followed the referee into the arena where several other competitors had already assembled.

The referee was brisk, reminding them all of the competition rules as they walked the course; what caused penalty points; what would get their dog eliminated. It was daunting for Neil. After all, up to now the training with Dotty and Sam had been rather like a shared game. This was definitely the real thing.

They began at the first jump — which because of its color and the shrubs decorating each side seemed much larger than their practice jumps. There were two tires: one like a "lollipop" on a pole, and another suspended inside a wooden frame, making it look smaller than it was. Fortunately Dotty would only need to jump through one of them, being a Junior.

There were two tunnels. A rigid one like their empty barrel, but also a long, collapsed one made of bright blue plastic.

Neil viewed it all with growing dismay.

"My Skip just loves these tunnels!" said a strident, confident voice beside him. Neil looked up into the face of an older boy wearing a bright sweatshirt with *Bingley Dog Agility Team* emblazoned across it.

"You've obviously done all this before," Neil said bleakly.

"Oh, yes. Since I was seven. I've trained four dogs so far, but Skip's the most promising. He's already got six silver trophies."

"Which class will you be in?"

"Veterans. We get the worst time handicap, unfortunately," said the boy. "Your first time?"

"Yes."

"Well, the trick is not to agitate your dog just because you're terrified. Let him go. They're not as bothered by all this as we are. Good luck!"

"Thanks," said Neil. At least Dotty didn't have to compete against this Skip.

They were just passing the seesaw, with its bright patches of yellow at each end. The referee was reminding them that their dog must touch the yellow contact points or be awarded a five-second penalty.

Then the weave. Dogs must work from right to left.

Here was the dog walk: a long plank up, then a bridge across two piles of bricks, and a long ramp down the other side. Contact points at each end. It looked huge.

Neil felt his mouth going dry. How could he have imagined being able to put Dotty through this — or even Sam?

The referee had stopped by a low table with a yellow square at its center.

"Your dog must jump on to this square and stay in the down position until the judge gives you the sign to carry on. Failure to stay down will result in a penalty . . ."

How long would Dotty have to stay down? She'd never manage it, Neil thought grimly. She just couldn't sit still for long.

The referee was talking again.

". . . and the course time for the Junior class is sixty seconds."

Sixty seconds! Neil groaned to himself. Maybe he should withdraw his entry now and avoid the humiliation of the mess he was going to make of all this.

*　*　*

Neil walked the Junior course one more time and then went dispiritedly to find his father and Emily.

"What do you think, Neil?" asked Mr. Parker, seeing his son's pale, troubled face.

"If I'd known how awful it was going to be, I'd never have started this. I'll never get Dotty around it. Certainly not in the time." He absently patted the dogs, who sensed his worry.

"It does look a bit . . . horrible," Emily admitted, looking over at the arena.

"Now, don't despair before you've even tried," said his dad. "This is a first time for both of you. You both need the experience. Dotty needs to show what she can do, and you need it to help Sam on his career. That is, if you want to go on with it."

"Of course I do!"

"Well, then, just do your best and let Dotty do hers! The Agility competition doesn't start for another hour," said Mr. Parker, "so let's go and see how Sarah's getting on with Fudge."

"Can we have a look around the booths, too?" asked Emily.

Mr. Parker nodded. "But after the tent," he said. "We don't want to miss the pet show."

They were just in time to see Fudge awarded ribbon for second prize. Sarah was delighted. She ran over to them, waving the ribbon happily. Carole Parker was behind her, carrying the hamster cage.

"Fudge was really good," Sarah said. "I put a

chocolate drop on the roof of his house and he climbed up and got it. Then he went through a tube to get another chocolate drop and he stood up at the bars to beg for more. Everyone thought he was really cute. That parrot only won because it could talk!"

A reporter was trying to take a photo of a lanky youth holding a colorful parrot. Neil laughed as the parrot flapped its wings and yelled at the reporter to "scram."

"I'd like a pet that talks," said Sarah, feeling just a tiny bit jealous of the attention the parrot was getting. "D'you think I could teach Fudge to talk, Mom?"

"I'm afraid not, Sarah." Her mother smiled. "Let's go and put Fudge in the car. He could use a nap after all that excitement." She and Sarah walked off toward the parking lot.

"Well, let's see if Dotty can beat Fudge's success," Mr. Parker said to Neil and Emily. "Come on, there's just time for a quick look around the booths before the big event."

Neil felt too nervous to join them.

"I'll go back with Dotty and watch the early events," he said. "The Junior competition doesn't come until the end." He left Emily, Sam, and his father heading for the long rows of booths and displays.

The Veteran class had already started in the Agility arena. As Neil arrived, he saw a German shepherd run into the ring with the boy he had met earlier.

"Please give a warm welcome to John Anderson and Skip!" boomed the loudspeaker.

The crowd applauded noisily.

The boy was right, thought Neil. Skip was a real pro. He shot around the obstacles like a bullet, enjoying every minute. He needed no encouragement to push his nose under the collapsed tunnel and worm his way through to the other side. John yelled at Skip to stay down on the table, but his dog was so excited that he jumped off before the judge gave the signal, which earned him a penalty. His total time was forty-five seconds.

Neil whistled softly in admiration. The course time for Veterans was fifty seconds.

He stayed by the rail with Dotty standing patiently beside him, watching the other experienced competitors take their turns. They weren't all as good as Skip by any means, and as Neil watched, caught up with the exhilaration of seeing dogs working so well, he could feel his earlier panic easing.

Some of the dogs had a real problem with the tires. That hole in the center must look very small to them, Neil figured. Others disliked the seesaw and jumped off the end before it touched the ground, missing the contact point.

In the Novice class, a golden retriever ran around the posts instead of weaving in and out of them. Another dog took two obstacles in the wrong order, so it was eliminated.

"Just do your best, Dotty," Neil said softly to the Dalmatian. She looked up at him and wagged her tail.

The rest of his family joined him at the rail. If they thought his task was impossible, no one mentioned it. Neil suspected that his dad had briefed them all in his absence.

"Oh, look at that dog!" said Sarah, pointing to the rough-coated collie mix currently running around the course. The animal showed no inclination at all to tackle any of the obstacles properly, but took them at random, inviting his owner to play when she started to get angry and shout at him to come to heel. Despite being eliminated early on, the dog led his owner and the referees on a wild chase before they could catch him.

The crowd was delighted. It was good to have a clown among all the serious professionals. Neil couldn't help wondering whether Dotty would behave the same way.

"I haven't seen the Hamleys yet, and it's almost Dotty's turn," said Emily. "What if they don't come?"

"I'm sure they will," said Mr. Parker.

But they still hadn't arrived when the Junior event was announced.

Neil couldn't help feeling relieved. Maybe it was best that they didn't see the mess he was going to make of the course. His stomach felt queasy, his palms cold and sticky.

"And now, ladies and gentlemen, we have the Junior event . . ." came the crackly announcement.

This was it. Was Dotty going to behave herself?

The first entry was a black Labrador. He had a clear round in sixty-two seconds.

Neil didn't have time to consider what that might mean.

"And now for Neil Parker from King Street Kennels with his Dalmatian — Dotty, the Puppy Patrol dog!" said the announcer cheerfully.

"Good luck, Neil!" said Emily as she patted him on the back.

"Come on, Dotty, we're on!" said Neil. As he led the Dalmatian into the ring, there was a round of applause. The whistle blew and Neil released Dotty's collar.

"Go, Dotty! *Go!*"

The Dalmatian went over the first jump.

"Good girl, Dotty," said Neil, running alongside her.

Up the ramp, along the top. Down the ramp — "Wait, Dotty!" — touch the yellow square. Off to the next.

Into the rigid tunnel — and out.

"Good girl, Dotty!"

Over another jump.

On to the seesaw. Down the other side. Touch the yellow square again.

Weave through the posts. "Careful, careful! Good girl!"

Neil was dimly aware of the crowd shouting encouragement, but he was so absorbed in keeping up with Dotty that his mind could focus on nothing else. Despite his own nerves, he drew some comfort from the fact that Dotty was really enjoying herself. She was obviously loving every minute, showing off what she did best.

She wasn't even fazed by the loudspeakers and their running commentary. How many penalties did she have? Had they followed the right order? Neil couldn't tell. He just wanted to get them both around.

The low table was the last obstacle.

Dotty almost overshot the yellow square, but Neil

managed to yell *"Down!"* in time to stop her from jumping off the other side. She obediently dropped like a stone and waited for his command to go.

Seconds ticked by. Neil willed the judge to signal before Dotty grew impatient, but just as the hand dropped, fate stepped in and snatched away his victory.

Like some weird nightmare in slow motion, Neil saw Dotty lift up her head toward the crowd. She stood up on the table, as if to get a better view, and before he could say "No!" she was off, galloping away into the crowd of people around the arena.

There were gasps of dismay from the watching crowd.

"Oh dear! Dotty's decided to take off," said the announcer. "What a shame. She was making such good time!"

Neil sprinted after her, calling desperately, deaf to sounds around him.

But Dotty ignored him.

He couldn't believe it. What had gotten into her?

But Dotty knew exactly what she was doing. Neil heard her barking with delight, and saw her jumping up at a pretty dark-haired lady, obviously expecting a baby very soon, and a man who seemed just as delighted to see Dotty as the dog was to see him.

Mr. Hamley and his wife. So that was it. Neil should have known.

"Hello, sir," said Neil, breathing heavily fro. chase. "I'm sorry."

Mr. Hamley looked up from patting Dotty and smiled rather sadly at Neil.

"Hello, Neil. This is my wife, Rachel." Neil shook hands politely with Mrs. Hamley. "You don't have to apologize. I had a feeling Dotty might do something like this, which is why we both kept a low profile. Not low enough, I'm afraid."

"But we did see how well she performed before she saw us, Neil," said Mrs. Hamley, smiling. "Dotty looked as if she was having the time of her life!"

"Yes, I think she was, " Neil admitted. "It was me that was scared stiff!"

"I'm not surprised," said Mr. Hamley, showing a rare touch of sympathy for Neil. "That course looked horrendous to me. You've done a great job getting her this far."

Hope soared in Neil. Maybe it had all been worthwhile after all. He looked at Mr. Hamley with shining eyes.

Dotty sensed something exciting and jumped up at Mr. Hamley.

"No, Dotty, down!" Neil said anxiously.

Mr. Hamley's jaw dropped in astonishment as Dotty promptly lay down at his feet, tongue lolling and tail wagging.

Just at that moment the Parkers arrived.

"You OK, Neil?" asked Mr. Parker. "Well, hello, Paul. And this must be Rachel. How do you do?"

Introductions were made, and it was decided that they should all go and get some refreshments before anymore serious discussions took place.

Over their cups of tea and coffee, Mr. Parker explained everything to the Hamleys, in particular his children's concern that Dotty would have to go away to a strange new home.

"I guessed much of that, Bob," Mr. Hamley admitted. "I could tell from the short time I've known Neil that his dogs are the most important things in his life and that he had grown very attached to Dotty. It didn't take much imagination to realize that your son would want to do the very best for her, and try and get Rachel and me to change our minds."

Neil's cheeks burned. Had it been so obvious? Neil stroked Dotty's head and couldn't speak. He sensed what Mr. Hamley was going to say next.

"Rachel and I are delighted Dotty has turned into such a lovely dog, but we can't alter our decision. It does mean, though, that she can go to her new home and we won't be worried all the time that she will be a nuisance. My friend Robert is coming up to get Dotty tomorrow, so you'll be able to meet him and give him advice on how best to look after her."

Their plan had failed.

CHAPTER TEN

"**W**ell, I guess that's it," Neil said sadly as the Hamleys left in the direction of the parking lot. He couldn't remember ever feeling this bad. "Can we go home now, Dad?"

The show was over as far as he and Dotty were concerned. All he wanted was to get back to King Street with her and Sam and make the most of the few hours they had left together. He'd probably never see her again.

Mr. Parker nodded and placed his arm reassuringly around Neil's shoulder. "You did your best, Neil. It's not your fault it didn't work out."

Suddenly someone pushed past, almost knocking them over. Neil struggled to keep his balance and his grip on Dotty's leash. The dogs barked furiously.

"Stop that thief!" a woman screamed from the crowd nearby. "He's got my purse!"

Neil turned round to see a young man running away, a black purse tucked under his arm. He was running through gaps in the crowds and heading toward one of the exit gates.

"Stop him! Thief!" the woman shouted hysterically.

A couple of men gave chase, but the thief had a good head start. He was going to get away.

Suddenly Neil heard Emily's determined voice behind him.

"Tackle the ball, Sam!" she yelled, sending the collie away from her. "Get the ball!"

Sam took off in pursuit like a streak of lightning.

Emily ran after him, shouting encouragement, and Neil, with his wits restored, followed with Dotty streaking along beside him, barking furiously.

Sam wove through the crowd, ignoring the shouts and yells, barking as he pursued his quarry.

The thief heard Sam and looked over his shoulder. Panic seized him when he saw the collie racing toward him and he quickly ran through the gate leading to the parking lot, slamming it shut behind him.

Sam cleared the gate in one easy bound.

Neil felt his lungs burning as he and Dotty ran faster and faster. They had overtaken Emily, who had been caught up in the crowd, and Neil was in time to see Sam fly over the gate. He was just close enough to witness Sam's party trick.

The collie shot in front of the startled thief, neatly tripping him up, and snatched the "ball" that fell from the youth's grasp. Without a second thought, Sam turned and leaped back over the gate with the purse in his mouth and ran to meet Neil with it. He dropped the bag at Neil's feet and backed away, barking, asking to play again.

Dotty leaped around with excitement, trying to snatch the purse herself. Fortunately, Emily arrived, very out of breath, and picked it up out of harm's way.

The dazed thief scrambled in the dirt to get up and escape, but as two security men from the parking lot opened the gate, Dotty ran past them and jumped up

at the thief. As the man staggered backward, wasting valuable seconds, he was grabbed by the men from security.

Neil was quick to control the excited dog. "Down, Dotty!" he ordered firmly.

The Dalmatian obeyed immediately and dropped down on all fours.

Neil knelt down and smothered Dotty and Sam with hugs and praise, digging in his pocket for a couple of biscuits as rewards, while Emily returned the purse to its delighted owner.

"Oh, thank you. Thank you," said the woman, clutching the purse to her chest. "What marvelous dogs you have! I'm so grateful. Wait till my husband hears about this!" She gave Sam and Dotty a pat, too.

There was quite a crowd around them now, eager to see and stroke the two dogs. Neil was bursting with pride, but felt a bit overwhelmed by all the attention. He was relieved to see his father and mother, with Sarah, making their way through the crowd toward him.

"Well done, both of you. That was quick thinking, Emily!" said Mr. Parker. "And well done, Sam!" He stroked the dog gently. "Good dog."

Emily beamed with pleasure.

"You should have seen Sam go!" she said. "It's all those soccer matches we've played! They were *both* so fantastic."

The reporter Neil had seen earlier at the pet show ran over to them. "This is going to make a great story," he said. "Let's get a shot of you and your sister with your dogs."

The reporter took photographs and then asked them questions, writing their answers swiftly in his notebook. He was interested to hear that Mr. and Mrs. Parker ran King Street Kennels.

"Great bit of training," he said. "And did you teach the other dog special things, too?"

"Yes!" said Emily, before Neil could reply. "Neil taught Dotty everything. She's going to be great! Only she's got to go away—"

She would have said a lot more, but her father coughed loudly. Standing on the edge of the crowd were Mr. and Mrs. Hamley, smiling at her.

"Oh!"

Mr. Hamley laughed. "It's all right, Emily. She's quite right," he said to the reporter. "Dotty is our dog and we left her in the care of King Street Kennels while we looked for a new home for her. She was just a bit too boisterous for us to manage. But I'm proud to say that Neil has done a remarkable job of training her, and I'd recommend him to anyone who has a difficult dog!" He explained how Dotty had come to be entered in the Agility competition. "We appreciate what you did, Neil, but we didn't need a ribbon to tell us that Dotty was special."

"And are you going to change your minds about keeping her?" asked the reporter matter-of-factly.

The Hamleys looked at each other.

Neil held his breath. He could see the hope shining in Emily's eyes.

The reporter looked up at the sudden silence.

"Was it something I said?" he asked.

Everyone laughed.

"The truth is," Mrs. Hamley spoke up, "Paul and I always knew that our home just wouldn't be the same without Dotty. When we saw her in the Agility arena, and then saw her break off just to come and join us, we knew that she missed us just as much. Now that we can see she can be controlled so well, too, we think her proper place *is* back with us. Would you like that, Dotty?"

Dotty looked as if her tail might fall off, it was wagging so hard. She almost knocked over the reporter, who laughed and had to catch his camera before it fell off his shoulder.

Neil and Emily let out whoops of joy. They hugged their parents, and the Parkers grinned and shook hands with the Hamleys.

The reporter was just putting his notebook away when a small group of show officials made their way through the crowd.

"Where's the dog that saved my wife's purse?" asked a tall, elderly gentleman in a hat and dark

suit. He had a red-and-gold badge on his lapel that read: EDWARD HARDING, CHAIRMAN.

"Over here, Mr. Harding!" said the reporter, snatching up his camera. "Can I have a picture of you, please, for the *Compton News*?" The flash lit up Mr. Harding's face before he could reply.

Mr. Harding shook hands with Neil and Emily and smiled. Then he looked at Sam and Dotty.

"Two delightful dogs you have here. Which one is the big hero?" he asked.

"Sam is, sir," said Neil. "He tackled the thief and brought the purse back to us."

"Well, I think that's splendid," said Mr. Harding.

"And to show how grateful we are, I'm going to present Sam with this special ribbon. For courage." He took a large red ribbon from his pocket and fixed it to Sam's collar. Sam lifted his paw and Mr. Harding shook it solemnly.

"Very well done, Sam."

The reporter's camera clicked and clicked.

Before they left the fairgrounds, the Hamleys arranged with Bob Parker for Paul to collect Dotty from the kennels the following morning.

The Parkers were making their way over to their own car, when Neil heard familiar voices shouting across the fairgrounds.

Chris and Hasheem caught up with them. Hasheem was struggling with an enormous pink toy rabbit he had won at one of the booths. They had seen everything that had happened.

"Sam's going to be famous," Chris said admiringly. "It was great the way he caught that thief. Must have a good soccer coach, eh, Sam?" He stroked Sam's head.

"I was sure Dotty was going to win the Agility contest, too," said Hasheem. "She looked like she had it sewn up. Man! Did you see her zip through the tunnel?" His hand swept down like a jet plane. "Zoom!"

"Yeah," Emily agreed. "She was doing great until

she saw Mr. Hamley and his wife." She sighed. "It's a shame — now we won't be able to collect the sponsor money for the SPCA because Dotty was eliminated."

"Hey, I'll still sponsor the Puppy Patrol," said Chris. "They both deserve the money after all they've done."

"So will I," said smiling Mrs. Smedley, who had just walked over to them as well. "Sam and Dotty did marvelously."

"And I will," said Tom Smedley, behind her. They both stopped to pat the dogs.

Emily was speechless with delight. Everything was working out perfectly!

Mr. Hamley arrived promptly the next morning to collect Dotty. He spent some time with Neil and his father while they gave him some useful advice about keeping Dotty in line.

"She's only a young dog, Paul," Bob reminded him, "and still learning. Once she gets older and wiser, she'll lose some of that boisterousness."

"I'm sure you're right, Bob," said Mr. Hamley. He turned to his dog, dancing impatiently at the end of her leash. "Well, Dotty, come on. Time to go home!"

They had only taken a few steps, though, before Mr. Hamley stopped and turned back to Neil and his dad. Sam was sitting quietly beside them.

"I almost forgot. I wanted to ask you, Neil, if you're still serious about Agility work? Or has yesterday changed your mind?" Neil's teacher had an expression on his face that Neil couldn't read. What was he getting at?

"No, it hasn't changed my mind, Mr. Hamley. I'm going to try again with Sam, and this time hopefully get it right."

"Well, if you think you might like to try again with Dotty, let me know."

"Oh, wow! Mr. Hamley!" Neil couldn't believe what his teacher was saying. "Do you mean it?"

"I certainly do. See you at the obedience class! Come, Dotty!"

Neil's dad stood beside him as they waved goodbye to Dotty and her owner. "Looks like you're going to steal away my business now, young man!"

Life at King Street Kennels went back to normal that week. At school, Neil had to suffer an embarrassing session in assembly, when the head teacher drew the attention of the entire school to the front-page article in the *Compton News* about the events at the county show and presented Neil with a leather-bound copy of *White Fang* by Jack London. But then things slipped into their usual routine, and Neil thought that he'd probably be famous until Friday if he was lucky.

Only one thing remained to be settled.

"Letter for you, Neil!" called his mother one morning.

Neil came down the stairs two at a time and snatched at the official-looking envelope lying on the kitchen table.

He ripped it open and pulled out a letter. A slip of paper edged in green fell out. Neil picked it up, his hand shaking slightly.

The Kennel Club, he read.

Registration certificate for: NEILSBOY PUPPY PATROL SAM. Owned by: Neil Parker.

There were other details, too, but Neil didn't see them.

"They chose it!" he shouted at his family, all looking at him as if he'd gone crazy. "They picked my first choice for Sam! Yeah!"

Sam charged into the kitchen when he heard Neil's shouts, looking for action.

"See that, Sam?" said Neil, waving the magic paper in front of the collie. "You're official. You can do anything now!"

He opened his arms with a whoop of happiness and Sam leaped into them and licked his face energetically.

"Neilsboy Puppy Patrol Sam: the name of a champion! Today, King Street! Tomorrow . . . the world!"